GREEN JUNGLE HELL

The Soviet RPD machine gun blasted into action and the Red Bears pressed forward, shouting in triumph. They leaped from cover to cover, drawing closer. With the RPD crew backing them up, they stood a good chance of breaching the Black Eagle line.

But Falconi's quick mind grasped the situation. He hit the transmit button on his Prick-Six. "Black Eagles!" he yelled. "Move to the center of the column. Eagle One! Eagle Two! *Go get 'em!*"

Falconi's men, mad with rage, charged into the clearing and the hell of flying bullets, mounting a shouting, bellowing counter-attack when there never should have been one.

FIRESTORM AT DONG NAM

THE BLACK EAGLES

14

BY JOHN LANSING

ZEBRA BOOKS
KENSINGTON PUBLISHING CORP.

Special Acknowledgement to Patrick E. Andrews

ZEBRA BOOKS

are published by

Kensington Publishing Corp.
475 Park Avenue South
New York, NY 10016

First printing: February 1988

Printed in the United States of America

This book is especially for
HUNKS IN SPACE
and the sardonic, sarcastic women who love 'em

THE BLACK EAGLES
ROLL OF HONOR
(Assigned or Attached Personnel Kill in Action)

Sergeant Barker, Toby — US Marine Corps
Sergeant Barthe, Eddie — US Army
Sergeant Bernstein, Jacob — US Marine Corps
First Lieutenant Blum, Marc — US Air Force
Sergeant Boudreau, Marcel — US Army
Chief Petty Officer Brewster, Leland — US Navy
Sergeant Carter, Demond — US Army
Master Sergeant Chun, Kim — South Korean Marines
Staff Sergeant Dayton, Marvin — US Army
Sergeant First Class Galchaser, Jack — US Army
Lieutenant Hawkins, Chris — US Navy
Sergeant Hodges, Trent — US Army
Mister Hosteins, Bruno — ex-French Foreign Legion
Petty Officer Second Class Jackson, Fred — US Navy
Chief Petty Officer Jenkins, Claud — US Navy
Specialist Four Laird, Douglas — US Army
Sergeant Limo, Raymond — US Army
Petty Officer Third Class Littleton, Michael — US Navy
Lieutenant Martin, Buzz — US Navy
Petty Officer Second Class Martin, Durwood — US Navy
Sergeant Matsamura, Frank — US Army
Staff Sergeant Maywood, Dennis — U.S. Army
Sergeant First Class Miskoski, Jan — US Army

Staff Sergeant Newcomb, Thomas – Australian Army

First Lieutenant Nguyen Van Dow – South Vietnamese Army

Staff Sergeant O'Quinn, Liam – US Marine Corps

Sergeant First Class Ormond, Norman – US Army

Sergeant Park, Chun Ri – South Korean Marines

Sergeant First Class Rivera, Manuel – US Army

Master Sergeant Snow, John – US Army

Staff Sergeant Taylor, William – Australian Army

Lieutenant Thompson, William – US Navy

Staff Sergeant Tripper, Charles – US Army

First Lieutenant Wakely, Richard – US Army

Staff Sergeant Whitaker, George – Australian Army

Gunnery Sergeant White, Jackson – US Marine Corps

ROSTER OF THE BLACK EAGLES
COMMAND ELEMENT

Lieutenant Colonel Robert Falconi
US Army
Commanding Officer
(14th Black Eagle Mission)

Petty Officer 1st Class Sparks Johnson
US Navy
Communications Chief

(2nd Black Eagle Mission)

Sergeant Gunnar Olson
US Army
Machine Gunner
(2nd Black Eagle Mission)

Specialist 4 Tiny Burke
US Army
Ammo Bearer
(2nd Black Eagle Mission)

Private Archie Dobbs
US Army
Detachment Scout
(12th Black Eagle Mission)

RAY'S ROUGHNECKS

First Lieutenant Ray Swift Elk
US Army
Team Leader/Executive Officer
(12th Black Eagle Mission)

Staff Sergeant Paulo Garcia
US Marine Corps
Auto Rifleman/Intelligence
(4th Black Eagle Mission)

Sergeant Dwayne Simpson
US Army
Grenadier

9

(3rd Black Eagle Mission)

Sergeant Jessie Makalue
US Army
Rifleman
(2nd Black Eagle Mission)

TOP'S TERRORS

Sergeant Major Top Gordon
US Army
Team Leader/Detachment Sergeant
(12th Black Eagle Mission)

Sergeant First Class Malcomb McCorckel
US Army
Auto Rifleman/Medic
(12th Black Eagle Mission)

Staff Sergeant Salty O'Rourke
US Marine Corps
Grenadier
(2nd Black Eagle Mission)

Petty Officer 3rd Class Blue Richards
US Navy
Rifleman/Demolitions
(7th Black Eagle Mission)

CALVIN'S CRAPSHOOTERS

Sergeant First Class Calvin Culpepper
US Army
Team Leader
(12th Black Eagle Mission)

Staff Sergeant Enrique Valverde
US Army
Auto Rifleman/Supply
(5th Black Eagle Mission)

Petty Officer 3rd Class Richard Robichaux
US Navy
Grenadier/Medic
(3rd Black Eagle Mission)

Sergeant Dean Fotopoulus
US Army
Rifleman
(2nd Black Eagle Mission)

Prologue

The lieutenant colonel, a muscular KGB man named Gregori Krashchenko, labored up the steep slope of the bare, rock-strewn Russian mountainside. This self-motivated physical ordeal was taking place in one of the most remote, desolate areas of the Caucasus Mountains of the Soviet Union.

Krashchenko was not dressed for a period of weekend jogging. Instead, he carried eighty pounds of field gear strapped to his brawny body and gripped a Sokolov heavy machine gun in his meaty fists. The weapon added another fifty-five pounds to the entire load his brawny body bore as he struggled upward toward the summit of the high hill. His thigh muscles burned with the effort and the air he sucked into his suffering lungs felt as if it were coming from a blast furnace.

Behind him, struggling to keep up, thirty

other men under similar circumstances suffered their own private physical agony. Sweat streamed down the pained expressions on their faces, and their limbs were wobbly from the supreme effort each labored under.

The group had begun the tortuous climb in a tight formation, but were now strung out a bit. The strongest were moving ahead of the pack at a gradual but steady pace.

These men, all young and tough, were volunteers for a special mission. Their detachment, officially listed by the proud name Red Bears, had numbered a hundred at the outset of this demanding program. But the rugged curriculum and endless hours of the harsh testing and training had finally whittled them down to these remaining thirty.

The candidates represented the cream of the Iron Curtain's elite forces. All were similar in appearance with their shaven heads, but the Red Bears' uniforms, though made of camouflaged-pattern material, differed slightly.

There were the green-and-tan splotches of the Soviet paratroops, the large brown-and-green blotches on gray preferred by Bulgarian mountain infantry, the green-and-brown spots on tan of the Russian naval infantry, and others that included East German, Czechoslovakian and Polish. The various qualifications badges sewn to the clothing attested to the soldiering skills of the wearers. These were professional soldiers as the insignia indicated. What couldn't be so apparently discerned was their fanatical devotion to the philosophies and aims of international communism.

All had endured three solid months of the brutal training in which bravery, physical endurance, and dedication were demanded of them. Nothing less would be tolerated in order to qualify for permanent membership in the Red Bears. The unit had already been slated for its first operation. This special mission that they had all opted to go on was one that their leader, Lt. Col. Gregori Krashchenko, considered sacred.

A quarter of a way up the mountain in this, their final test, five of them collapsed. The quintet had reached the absolute end of their physical endurance. All muscle and nerve control was now gone. Broken in heart as well as body, these despondent failures knew they were out of the unit at that point. That left twenty-five to continue the struggle that could earn them a spot in Krashchenko's special detachment.

Three more gave it up at the half way point. The other twenty-two, some now staggering from nearly unbearable pain and fatigue, approached the two-thirds mark where two more went down from the torture.

Krashchenko turned and now ran backward as a display of his fantastic physical condition brought on by the iron-hard regimen to which he had submitted himself after accepting the challenge of commanding such a unit.

"Step out, you dolts!" he bellowed. "You mother's sons! Show me you're more steel than flesh and blood if you wish to bear the proud title of

Red Bear!"

Partly in anger, partly in fear, the candidates forced themselves to increase their efforts.

Fifteen more minutes found them near the top. But it was still too much for another four. One, coughing blood, went face down. He valiantly pushed himself up and stared forlornly at Krashchenko standing a few meters higher. He instinctively reached out his hand, not in a gesture of asking for help, but rather as a sign of seeking forgiveness from an admired and respected man he felt he had failed. Then his eyes rolled and he once more collapsed onto the barren earth. Only a final superhuman desire on his part allowed him to roll over and die looking up into the sun.

When Krashchenko reached the summit, he stopped to watch the others reel like drunken men toward him. Finally, gasping but managing to smile despite the pain their bodies felt, they joined the KGB officer.

Krashchenko looked at the sixteen survivors. He raised the machine gun over his head in triumph. "Congratulations, comrades!" he shouted in his guttural voice. "You have proven that you are the best of the best. You will be awarded the heroic title of Red Bears. Your physical courage and stamina have earned you the right to continue on this mission of honor for international communism!"

Soaked in sweat, close to tears, and now barely able to move their cramping muscles, the volunteers managed to imitate their leader by pushing their own machine guns over their heads and emitting a cheer.

"In only a few weeks," Krashchenko exclaimed in a near frenzy, "you will be with me in southeast Asia to hunt down and kill Robert Falconi and his Black Eagle gangsters!"

The group shouted as one in unison. *"Da Tovarisch Podpolkovnik! Rasrushat Chernie Orel!* — Kill the Black Eagles!"

Chapter 1

Chuck Fagin popped open his attache case and slipped his Black Eagle file inside. He closed the cheap, vinyl cover and snapped shut the one lock that worked. After quickly tossing down the half-finished Irish whiskey and soda he'd mixed himself a scant five minutes previously, he walked to the door of his office and stepped out into the reception area.

Andrea Thuy, the beautiful Eurasian woman who held a captaincy in the ARVN (Army of the Republic of Vietnam — the South Vietnamese army), looked up from her own desk. "Ready to go, Chuck?" She had recently been reassigned as his administrative assistant after a lengthy absence.

"I'm ready," Fagin answered. "Everything I need is here," he added indicating the attache case.

"My God!" Andrea exclaimed. "Do you still have *that* thing?"

Puzzled, Fagin looked at the piece of battered luggage. "Sure. It's still got a lot of good years' use left."

The young woman was dressed in a neatly tailored set of American jungle fatigues that bore ARVN rank insignia. She picked up her own briefcase, a smart leather affair with a combination lock, and stepped out from her desk. Still feminine despite her martial apparel, she gave her boss a close visual inspection. She slowly shook her head and displayed a disapproving frown.

"Hey!" Fagin exclaimed defensively. "What's wrong?"

Andrea smiled slightly. "I didn't say anything."

"Hell, you didn't have to," Fagin retorted. "It's all in that expression on your pretty face."

"Why, Chuck," she said soothingly. "Just because your striped tie doesn't match your checkered shirt or your suit looks like it's been slept in for three nights running, and there's cigar ashes all over the front of the whole outfit, doesn't mean I disapprove of your attire."

"I don't recall any need for a full-dress inspection," Fagin scowled. "Are we going to a special staff meeting or to the General's Ball, huh?"

"You're right," Andrea said. But she couldn't resist walking over and brushing the ashes off the lapel of his dumpy jacket. "Let's go to the meeting without any more comments, okay?"

"That's more like it," Fagin said. "Jesus, you're a typical goddamned woman, Andrea. What a nag! That's one of the reasons I never married!"

Andrea winked at him. "A good wife would do wonders for you, Chuck-O."

"And stop calling me 'Chuck-O'. It sounds like I'm a clown on a kiddie TV show or something."

"Whatever you say," Andrea said with an impish grin.

The two stepped out of the doorway and walked past the MP guard stationed there. A couple of years previously the couple had run the paperwork side of the Black Eagle detachment as a team for several months. Their administrative teamwork had kept the paperwork and logistics side of Black Eagle operations running smoothly and efficiently.

Andrea had actually begun her career with this clandestine outfit as a full-fledged fighting member, but a love-affair with its commander, Lt. Col. Robert Falconi, had caused her to be removed from active field service. She'd returned to combat on only two occasions. Once when she was needed as a ploy to convince Chinese mercenaries to continue serving the anti-communist cause. In that particular caper, she actually played the part of a Chinese war goddess that had come to life. The second and most recent had been on the Black Eagles' last operation when she went into action to act as a guide on the detachment's latest operation which took place in the same area of North Vietnam where she'd grown up as a child.

In reality, there had been one other time when Andrea had left the office for the field. But that instance had certainly not been voluntary. Red agents, ferreting out her relationship with the tough Black Eagle, had kidnapped her and taken her north for interrogation and eventual execution. Falconi led the rescue effort that brought her back to freedom but only after she'd suffered a long term of mental and physical torture. She had been sent to the States for a period of psychological treatment to rid her of the effects of the horrible experience. Now she was back in the fold, again aiding Chuck Fagin in running the front office for the toughest team of jungle fighters in Southeast Asia.

But Chuck Fagin, strongly suspecting she was still deeply in love with Robert Falconi, was making sure she would not return to the field after the last foray. He wanted a long term of close-up observation to see if she was still infatuated with the handsome commanding officer. And that went both ways too. Even though the two didn't show any romantic inclination toward each other during the weeks in North Vietnam, Fagin was not convinced that the fire of romantic love had died out. His unusually polite and mild inquiries had been met with indifferent denials by both Falconi and Andrea. This left the CIA man even more confused about their true relationship.

Fagin and Andrea arrived at an elevator and had their IDs checked by another MP. Then they stepped aboard the conveyance and pressed the button for the third floor—the top one—in the building that housed the Special Operation Group's headquarters.

The doors opened and they stepped out for yet another security routine foisted on them by one more tough military policeman. Again with identity documents carefully scrutinized, they went down the hall to a door which, like all the others, bore no markings indicating the office inside. But Fagin needed no signs. He knew exactly which office it was as he knocked.

A bald, swarthy brigadier general answered the summons. "Hi ya, Fagin. Hello, Captain Thuy. Come on in and make yourselves at home. Care for a drink?" He pointed to the well-stocked wet bar across the room. "It's all yours."

"Thanks. I could do with a soda," Andrea said. "What about you, Chuck?"

"Irish whiskey on the rocks," Fagin answered.

The general, an airborne ranger named Taggart, laughed. "I got scotch, Fagin. That's the closest I have to spirits from Erin."

"Okay," Fagin said. "Then scotch it is."

The general ignored his desk. He took an easy chair situated close to a leather sofa. He was already working on a gin-and-tonic. He sipped it while waiting for his guests to situate themselves with their own libations and get comfortable on the couch before he spoke. "Are the Black Eagles out at their field garrison in Nui Dep?"

"No," Fagin answered. "They're on R&R here in Saigon. They're out in the isolation barracks. As a matter of fact, I'm hoping to arrange having them stay here in Saigon for quite awhile." He looked suspiciously at the general. "You know that."

23

"I just needed a confirmation," Taggart said. "What shape are they in?"

"Both on the physical and morale sides, they're top notch," Fagin said. "They came off the last operation without a casualty." He indicated Andrea with a nod of his head. "The pretty cap'n here was with 'em."

Taggart winked at her. "I'll bet you did a hell of a job."

"I can pull my weight," Andrea said, unsmiling. "And we accomplished our mission. We destroyed a Red communications interference center."

"Well done," Taggart said. "What's the operational strength of Falconi's detachment?"

Fagin did some figuring in his head. "There are seventeen of 'em, General. Falconi has the detachment broken down into four teams." He displayed a quizzical expression. "Why?"

"I'll get to that later," Taggart said. "This is a bit awkward to explain." He stood up and began to pace slowly back and forth in front of the two guests as he spoke slowly and thoughtfully. "Fagin, you're well aware of the true relationship between our intelligence services and those of the Soviets, aren't you?"

"Sure," Fagin answered. "I damned well ought to be after all these years of clandestine operations. Hell, I've done everything from courier work to taking out some particularly nasty bastard."

"Right. And you're well aware that we have a line of communications—a rapport, if you will—with them," the general continued. "It's not always friendly, but sometimes one of our operatives runs into one of theirs. If there's no real clash of purposes at that particular moment, it becomes a kind of hands-off thing where we do our thing and they go about their business."

Fagin laughed. "Hell, yes! I was on a case in Austria a few years back. I ran into a KGB guy I'd known during the partisan operations in the Balkans during World War II. We even had a drink together for old times' sake."

"Sure," the general said. "Nothing unusual in that. We get together for prisoner swaps, special deals, and we've even helped each other out when it was advantageous to both sides in Third World countries."

Andrea was getting impatient. "What you're saying, General, is that in the real world we have contact and talk together, right?"

"Yeah, Captain Thuy," Taggart said. "That's exactly what I mean to say—we *communicate.*" He pronounced the word very carefully and with a great deal of emphasis.

Fagin, as sharp mentally as he was sloppy physically, pulled out a cigar and lit it. "So. I presume we've been—" He hesitated and imitated the general. "—*communicating.*"

"Exactly," Taggart said. "The KGB has made contact with the CIA and a deal has been proposed and accepted."

"A deal?" Fagin asked. "It must be out of the ordinary or you wouldn't have called us in here."

Andrea was also a couple of steps ahead. "And it must also affect the Black Eagles."

"This thing deals entirely with the Black Eagles," Taggart said. He paused and took a deep breath. "For the fact of the matter is, the KGB has called for a showdown between the Black Eagles and the Red Bears."

"The Red Bears?" Andrea asked.

"They're the Iron Curtain's equivalent of Falconi's group," Taggart explained. "This particular group is led by a fellow we're all familiar with. He is Lieutenant Colonel Gregori Krashchenko."

"Krashchenko!" Fagin yelled out. "He's the rottenest sonofabitch ever produced by a totalitarian society. Could outdo Hitler in pure meanness if the situation was right."

"You're absolutely correct about that," Taggart agreed. He went over to the bar and mixed another gin. He returned to the conversation after a stiff gulp. "The situation is this: Krashchenko's superiors have contacted their counterparts in the CIA and have issued a challenge. They want to pit the Red Bears against the Black Eagles in a neutral zone. Winner take all—loser die."

"A neutral zone?" Fagin asked. "Where for God's sake?"

"In Southeast Asia," Taggart said.

Andrea protested. "We can't trust them!"

"They won't cheat," Taggart said. "For them to break the rules would be an admission to us that their Red Bears are second-rate. For us to do so would be to admit that the Black Eagles can't win on their own either."

"Rules?" Andrea exclaimed. *"Rules?* This is being treated like a ball game of some sort."

"I suppose it is," Taggart said. "But the conditions are simple. Both detachments will be of equal strength. They will enter the battle zone and not be able to make contact with their own side again until they walk out."

"What about the wounded?" Fagin asked. "Will there be medavac for them?"

Taggart shook his head. "No."

"And re-supply?" Andrea demanded.

"None," Taggart flatly stated. "Each side will have only what they take in with them."

"What's the method of infiltration?" Fagin inquired.

"A simultaneous daylight parachute drop at opposite ends of the battle zone," Taggart said.

"Our guys can use equipment bundles," Andrea said.

But the general shook his head. "Nope. And there will be inspections teams on site for boarding the aircraft. We'll observe them and they'll check us out."

Now it was Fagin who paced the room. "Goddamn it! I don't like this one damned bit." He glared at Taggart. "You can't order them to do this."

"Of course not," Taggart said. "It will be purely voluntary." He paused. "Of course the Red Bears are already primed and raring to go."

"The bastards!" Andrea hissed through her clenched teeth.

"I find it hard to believe our big shots would go

for this," Fagin said. "Even if there are tons of communication between East and West."

"Our side agreed," Taggart said. "And if this doesn't come off, the world-wide intelligence community will know about it too."

"But it won't be in the newspapers," Andrea protested.

"Of course not," Taggart said. "But the next time the CIA wants to recruit an agent, or organize some counter-espionage, they'll have trouble because our reputation will be badly warped. The word will be that we backed down from the Soviets out in the cold."

"Out in the cold?" Andrea said aloud to herself.

"Yeah," Taggart said. "You know—in the field in operating areas."

"I know what it means!" Andrea snapped.

Fagin grimaced. "That could spell disaster for several clandestine projects. Potential agents would be afraid our side wouldn't have the guts to back 'em up or pull 'em out of a hairy situation."

Andrea was silent for several long seconds before she spoke again. She was a completely trained, seasoned, and tested operative in her own right. She smothered whatever emotional reaction she had to the idea. "You're correct. No doubt."

"It's still voluntary on the Black Eagles' part," Taggart reminded them. "This thing isn't etched in stone yet."

"I'll have a meet with Falconi," Fagin said. "And I'm not sure he'll go for it. There have been thirty-six Black Eagles killed so far. Falconi has wept inside for each and every one of 'em."

"Yes," Andrea added. "And those guys were lost on tactically meaningful combat operations. This latest thing is just—just—"

"Pride," Taggart added.

"Men have died for less in the past," Fagin said.

"And more will in the future," Taggart said.

Fagin finished his drink and set the glass down on the bar. "Okay, Taggart. I'll go talk to Falconi and bring your answer back tomorrow afternoon."

"Be here at 0800 in the morning," Taggart said. He walked to the door and opened it for them. "It was nice talking with you."

Andrea frowned and she led Fagin out of the office. "I can't say the same."

Chapter 2

Private Archie Dobbs lethargically pushed the broom down the aisle between the row of bunks. He performed this chore with an expression on his face that was as blank as his mind at that particular moment. If he'd wanted some mental exercise, he could have pulled up some pretty exciting memories about the particular building he was in at the moment.

This was the isolation center at Tan Son Nhut Air Base. Located in an area set aside for SOG's special airborne operations, it was well-guarded and out of the way of other installations on the sprawling complex. An ARVN infantry unit, made up of purely defensive weapons, including heavy machine guns and mortars, surrounded the place. It was here that Archie had first joined the Black Eagles after being put out of a

Saigon whorehouse by no less a personage than Lt. Col.—then a captain—Robert Falconi himself. During their first night in the billets, a fanatical Viet Cong urban guerrilla group launched a suicide attack against the barracks. The Reds swept through the ARVN defenses like a hot knife through butter. They pinned down Falconi and his men with devastating firepower. Only determination and desperation of their own had turned the day.

But that was a couple of years back. Now the glory was temporarily gone while Archie pulled clean-up detail at this scene of an old victory. The reason behind Archie's low rank and his menial job assignment was the fact of a severe punishment he was enduring under the auspices of Sgt. Maj. Top Gordon. Less than a month ago, Archie had been a fully-ranked staff sergeant with all privileges and monies entitled to him, but a fall from grace had occurred which brought about his demotion all the way down the United States Army's rank structure. And his punishment hadn't stopped there. He was also handed a solid six-month confinement to quarters.

Archie had gone AWOL—Absent Without Leave—because of a "Dear John" letter his girl friend Betty Lou Pemberton had sent him. Betty Lou, a second lieutenant in the Army Nurse Corps, sent him this sad missive of dismissal from her favors, and Archie had responded by impetuously taking off without permission from the Black Eagles' forward base camp at Nui Dep. Normally he would have been given a damned

31

good ass-chewing for such a rash action, but the stunt had caused him to miss going on an operation with the detachment. Although he had rejoined them during a resupply parachute drop, the sergeant major was damned good and pissed off.

Hence, Private Dobbs now swept the quarters where he and his buddies — now whooping it up in Saigon bars — were billeted while they enjoyed a bit of well-deserved Rest & Recreation after a tough mission up in North Vietnam.

The sound of a jeep's motor outside caught Archie's ear. He walked over to the window and looked out. SFC Malpractice McCorckel got out of the vehicle and fetched something from the back. He walked up toward the small barracks building.

Archie, glad for company, went to the door. "Hi ya, Malpractice!" he called out. "What's happening, good buddy? Did you come to visit for awhile?"

"Nope," Malpractice answered. "I ain't got the time." He came inside carrying a cheap but large styrofoam cooler. "But I brung you some beer."

"Hey, thanks," Archie said. "I could sure use some cold suds. You gonna stay and down a few with me? Hell, I bet you can at least spare a few minutes to jaw with a pal, can't you, Malpractice? What do you say?"

"I can't do it," Malpractice said. "Jean's waiting for me." Jean, his wife, was a Vietnamese nurse who had helped Malpractice in his medical duties during the detachment's actions on the Song Cai

River. Really named Xinh, Malpractice had started calling her by the English name. "Me and Jean are having Top over for supper."

"You've done a lot for that guy," Archie said. He referred to the fact that the couple had operated on the sergeant major and saved his life during emergency battle surgery in the field. "And you're feeding him too."

"Yeah," Malpractice said. He set the beer down. "Sorry you can't get out, Archie."

"Yeah, me too," Archie said. "But I asked for it."

"Yeah, you sure as hell did," Malpractice stated flatly. "I guess that really screwed up your love life."

"Tell me about it," Archie said. "The only chance I get to talk with Betty Lou is when I go over to the PX. Top lets me call her from there."

"Too bad," Malpractice said. "I'd really like to stick around and bullshit for awhile, but there ain't much time. Jean is waiting, so I gotta go, Archie. I'll see you later, okay?"

"Okay, man," Archie said. "Thanks for the beer. How much do I owe you?"

"Oh, nothing," Malpractice said. "All the guys chipped in."

"What a great bunch!" Archie said sincerely.

"Yeah," Malpractice agreed. "Well, I'll see you later." He gave a wave and went out the door.

Archie pulled his P-38 can-opener from his pocket and opened up the beer. Feeling very lonely, he took a deep swallow and listened to Malpractice drive away.

Bar girls screamed in horror and ran out the door. The little sex-pots crashed into the crowd of curious onlookers who had gathered outside the saloon.

Inside, leaning up against the bar, Marine Staff Sgt. Paulo Garcia hunched his muscular shoulders and punched straight out. His fist landed square on the face of a merchant seaman, propelling the man backward across the room.

Tiny Burke, all six-foot, four inches and two hundred and twenty pounds of solid muscle, had a civilian sailor in each arm. The big kid, the official ammunition bearer of the Black Eagles, emitted a roar and with all the speed he could muster, charged toward a back booth. When he judged the distance right, he released the two unfortunate guys. They continued forward to crash into the bar furniture, turning it into a pile of split lumber.

His best buddy, Gunnar the Gunner Olson, danced and feinted around another seaman. "C'mon! C'mon!" Gunnar taunted the guy. "Let's see how goddamned bad you are."

The civilian smiled and swung a round house left that collided hard with the side of Gunnar's head. "*Fy da!*" he exclaimed in Norwegian as he lumbered awkwardly to his right and tried to keep his balance. But he slipped and fell on the slippery floor.

"Now you'll get yours, asshole!" his opponent yelled. He moved forward to deliver a kick, but suddenly found himself with his feet off the floor.

Tiny Burke held onto the guy. "Hey! Don't you kick my little buddy!"

The seaman twisted his head and looked up into the big kid's face. He smiled. "Okay."

Tiny set him down. "Now that's nice."

The civilian suddenly threw a straight punch into Tiny's stomach. It was like hitting a brick wall.

"Oh!" Tiny said. "Now *that* ain't nice." He swung an overhead bolo and brought it straight down on top of the sailor's head. The man's eyes rolled upward and he collapsed into a heap at the ammo carrier's feet. "Bad man!" Tiny admonished him.

Blue Richards, who had just sent one of the merchant marines sailing out the front door, sprinted back into the action. He leaped from a chair to a table, then dove out over the brawling throng emitting a wild Rebel yell.

"Yaaaaaa-hooooooo!"

He missed the guys who were wildly raising holy hell with each other in the riot, and sailed over them in a somewhat graceful dive. But the free flight ended and Blue crashed straight into Doc Robichaux who had been mixing it up with another guy. Both Black Eagles crashed to the floor in front of the confused man. The seaman leaned over and looked at Blue with a puzzled expression on his face. "Whose side are you on, pal?"

Blue, looking up, delivered a solid uppercut that put out the guy's lights. He struggled to his

35

feet. "I am on the side of God and Right and the American Way!" he exclaimed in a rush of drunken patriotism.

A chair crashed into him and he fell down, landing on Doc who had been trying to stand up again. Doc rolled him off. "Do me a favor, Blue," he begged. "Go stand in the corner for awhile, okay?"

Whistles suddenly blew outside and were followed within seconds by a group of American MPs and Vietnamese civilian police who charged *en masse* through the bar door.

Both sides in the brawl now had a common goal—escape. Nobody wanted to spend the rest of the night in jail. A spontaneous rush for the sidewalk by all participants bowled over the representatives of the law. The melee built up, then the Black Eagles—Gunnar the Gunner, Paulo Garcia, Blue Richards and Doc Robichaux—squeezed out of the mass of bodies and popped free to join the crowd outside.

They turned and looked back at the mini-riot going on inside. "Wow!" Doc said. "Some goings-on, huh?"

"Yeah," Blue said grinning. "It's fun to come into town and relax awhile, ain't it?"

Sgt. Maj. Top Gordon, wearing a freshly laundered and starched set of khakis, waited as Jean McCorckel set the plate of hamburgers and french fried potatoes in front of him.

"The cook at the PX taught me this recipe that

you Americans like so much," she said proudly. "Take a bite, Top. You like?"

Top grinned and picked up one of the hamburgers. The bun was freshly heated and the meat patty inside was crisp on the outside with a perfect pale-red interior. He sampled it like a gourmet checking out chateaubriand. "Mmmm!" he said chewing. "Perfect."

Malpractice, now served as well, grinned. "I tried to get her to fix steaks, Top. But she swears that this is the food we like the best."

"Of course," Jean said, sitting down. "I see what GIs eat in snack bar." As a nurse she was employed in one of the convalescent hospitals at Long Binh and had great opportunity to view Americans first hand.

Top winked at her. "You made the best choice, Jean," he said.

Jean glowed with pleasure. "You see?" she said to her husband. "I know best."

"You've learned a lot of English since you came down from Tam Nuroc," Top said. He referred to her home village on the Song Cai River.

"Thank you, Top," Jean said. "I am encouraged to study. They give to me two hours every day to learn your language."

"Say, Top," Malpractice interjected. "I guess I forgot to tell you. She works with Archie Dobbs' girl friend over in one of the convalescent wards."

"Yes," Jean said. "Too bad about Archie being bad soldier. Betty Lou is so sorry. She thinks it be her fault."

"No way," Top said. "Archie pulled a dumb

stunt. Now he's paying the price."

Jean suddenly stood up. "Oh! I forget the beer." She went out to the kitchen and returned with cold bottles of Budweiser. "My Malcomb told me this your favorite, Top."

Top laughed. "Well, your Malpractice—whoops, I mean Malcomb—was right."

Jean sat down again. "I see Americans like chocolate milk shake with burgers. But you like beer better."

"Yeah," Top said. "I guess I'm just a funny old geezer."

The three settled down to their meal, an oasis of calm and friendship in a stormy desert of war.

Lt. Col. Robert Falconi, taking care of the bottle of wine he carried, stepped out of the taxi and paid the driver. He had taken the cab to an area of Saigon known as *Le Quartier des Colons*.

Although this part of town was not an actual political department or zone, it had a name all its own because of the nationality of most of the people who lived there. These were voluntary expatriates of metropolitan France. After the armistice that established the two Vietnams, many had gone back to France once, but after years in the colonial service, they discovered they were strangers too far removed from old customs and traditions to become regular Frenchmen again. They were *colons*—now and forever. Most of them, though only a step or two above poverty, lived in the past, during a time of colonial grandeur and authority when they were the rulers of this humid, hot land.

There was another resident in that section of the city. Andrea Thuy preferred the quiet neighborhood with its quasi-French street cafes and the quaint old loafers who hung around them drinking cheap wine and talking of the good old days.

There were memories here for Robert Falconi too. But these were not of past glories, they were of a past romance. He and Andrea had been lovers once. He had lived with her in the same apartment he now headed for as he ascended the rickety stairs in the old apartment house. Although he walked at a steady pace, there was some feelings of uncertainty in his manly chest. What he was doing had not been carefully thought out. In fact, he had decided to come visiting while in the middle of his fifth straight bourbon at the Tan Son Nhut officers club.

Falconi reached the door and shifted the bottle of wine. It took him a couple of more moments to make up his mind. For one single second, he almost turned and walked away. Now he took a deep breath and knocked.

The door opened slowly. Andrea looked at him, her almond-shaped eyes betraying her surprise. "Robert!"

"Hi," Falconi said. He hesitated. "Hell, I guess I should've called."

"No, no," she assured him. "Please come in."

Suddenly all romantic notions and urges Falconi had been feeling vanished with the sound of the male voice in the other room. "Who is it, Andrea?"

Chuck Fagin stepped out into the small foyer. He grinned. "Hi ya, Falconi. What's new, kid?"

Chapter 3

The official international language for air traffic controllers is English. This is a world-wide working arrangement, so that no matter whether the airport is in Madrid, Paris or Cairo, the men monitoring the flight patterns speak the English language.

The lingo used in the control tower at Hanoi is most definitely not the mother tongue of Britain – the people on duty there speak Russian.

And it was crisp Russki words with a Vietnamese accent that directed the large Soviet AN-12 transport to begin its descent and turn onto an approach of 170 degrees through the rapidly darkening sky of dusk.

The pilot in the aircraft cranked the flaps down and raised the spoilers on top of the wings to break up the flow of air over the plane. When the big transport immediately slowed, the airman gently throttled back the four turboprop engines almost halving the top speed of 300 knots. The runway lights now came on and he flew toward them, working the rudders as he lined up on the double row of illumination to his lower front. This action caused his flying machine to yaw a bit more on course, then settled down for the final run in.

The anti-aircraft crew at the edge of the large airport could barely see in the gloom. But they still waved at the big red stars on the transport as it roared in and touched down less than a hundred meters from their position. The airplane's brakes squealed and the engines roared in reverse to slow it enough for manageable taxiing, then the pilot guided it past the main terminal. He spotted the little command car in front of him that had a sign on the back reading: *SPEDOVTA NRAVITSYA*. It was polite, but incorrect, Russian for PLEASE FOLLOW.

The aviator did exactly that, letting the vehicle lead him across the wide arterial network of runways to a guarded gate. They rolled through the wide portal and into a totally secure area.

The place was a mini-aerodrome within the larger one, being complete with a hangar and refueling facilities. Then the engines were cut, and the big hydraulic controls came into action lowering the ramp in the back of the aircraft.

Inside, Lt. Col. Gregori Krashchenko, commander of the Red Bears, stood in front of his men. "Now, comrades," he announced to them. "You will step out on the soil of North Vietnam. This nation, who is the brave little friend of the European communists, is fighting the evil neo-imperialism of the American gangsters and their running dogs of the south!" Turning and gesturing dramatically, he led his men down the ramp.

This experience, which promised to be exhilarating at first, proved to be slightly disappointing to the Red Bears. They didn't exactly step out on the "soil" of North Vietnam. Instead they found themselves treading the concrete of a runway apron.

But it was a homecoming of sorts for Krashchenko. He had been stationed in Hanoi for more than two years as he directed a futile war against Falconi's Black Eagles. This task was conducted from special offices in the general headquarters building of the North Vietnamese Army. Despite the best facilities, agent control and communications, Krashchenko had failed.

Back for this new attempt, the Russian strode across the runway and almost missed a step when he sighted his former aide who had served him in his GHQ office. Despite their common cause and professional relationship, the Russian detested the man almost as much as Robert Falconi. This person was North Vietnamese Army officer Truong.

The sight of this fellow communist soldier brought back stinging memories of insults at failed missions and the humiliation of failure in front of a man that Krashchenko felt was a racial inferior.

Truong marched boldly up to the Russian. He did not salute. "Hello, Comrade Lieutenant Colonel Krashchenko." His voice was haughty and

43

close to being outright disrespectful. "Welcome back to Hanoi—your home away from home."

Krashchenko started to bellow at him about proper military courtesy until he noted the man's epaulets. Where there had been two stripes with the single star of a major, there were now two additional stars. Now outranked, it was Krashchenko who saluted. "Greetings, Comrade Colonel."

"As I said, *Tovarisch Podpolkovnik,* welcome back to Southeast Asia," Truong said. He glanced at the men behind Krashchenko. Lean and tough, they had donned their heavy field gear and silently formed up into a squared-away military formation. "You have brought impressive troops with you. They seem well-drilled."

Krashchenko grinned evilly. "They do more than march pretty, Comrade Colonel Truong."

"Yes," Truong said. "I am aware of your mission. In fact, I have been assigned as a liaison of sorts for you." He tapped his shoulder boards. "I now have more rank in order to get things done faster."

"So I noticed," Krashchenko said coldly. Then he added insincerely. "My heartiest congratulations to you. I am sure this promotion reflects your undying and complete devotion to world socialism."

Truong knew the words were so much bullshit, but he loved hearing them from Krashchenko just the same, because he knew they stuck in the Russian's craw. "I have arranged transportation for your unit," the NVA colonel said. "The trucks are waiting on the other side of the hangar."

"I will move my men over there," Krashchenko said. He made a snappy turn and marched to the head of his small command. *"Vinmani!"* he barked. "Shoulder, arms! Right, turn! Forward, march!" He positioned himself beside them and counted out the cadence as they marched. *"Odin! Dva! Tri! Chetireh! Levaya! Levaya!"*

The men, although of different Iron Curtain nationalities, fully understood the commands. And they now all sported the same style of uniform. Each Red Bear was clothed in the green and yellow mottled design of the Soviet paratroops' lightweight summer combat uniform. Complete with a hood that could be drawn over the head to add more camouflage, the overall type garb sported an insignia showing a frontal view of a snarling bear face that was sewn over the right breast pocket. Although this spoiled the natural color of the clothing, the men had arranged its placement so the shoulder harnesses of their web gear did not cover it.

Truong could not fail to notice the colorful devices. "The insignia of your unit is most interesting," he said. "But the bright scarlet of its design will attract attention, will it not?"

Krashchenko kept his eyes straight ahead. "Of course, Comrade Colonel. We have arranged it in this manner so that it will be last thing seen by each and every Black Eagle — as he dies."

Robert Falconi sat up in the bed and reached

over on the nightstand for his cigarettes. He fumbled in the weak light coming into the room off the street lamp outside. It was a couple of moments before he finally grasped the pack. A minute later he had lit one and slowly exhaled a puff of smoke.

The ceiling fan above turned slowly, sending gentle wafts of artificial wind that brought a small but significant degree of relief from the strong tropical heat.

Andrea Thuy, in bed beside him, stirred. Slowly awakening, she looked up and winced sleepily. "Robert, darling, I wish you'd give that up. They are beginning to speak seriously of smoking as a cause of cancer and disease of the heart."

Falconi answered by taking another drag.

Now Andrea sat up. "God! You're a stubborn man, Robert."

"Go on, admit it. That's the biggest part of my attraction to you," he said.

"It is not," Andrea said. She yawned, then stifled a smile. "You were really surprised to see Fagin here when you showed up, weren't you?"

"Not half as surprised as at what he told me," Falconi said.

"Weren't you even a tiny bit jealous, my love?" she asked.

"Hell, no!"

Andrea playfully nudged him. "Come now, darling, admit that you thought we were lovers. You really did, didn't you?"

Falconi laughed. "With Fagin?"

"He has—" Andrea hesitated, then added, "—a certain charm, Robert."

"Sure," Falconi said. "About like one of those cobras that slither around the jungle out there."

"You're horrid. Did you know that?"

Falconi didn't answer. He finished off the cigarette and ground it out in the ashtray. He was thinking, but it wasn't about Fagin being at the apartment. "When did you two find out about this proposed mission against the Red Bears?"

"Earlier today," Andrea said. She knew he was deeply concerned. "Fagin didn't like it. He argued with General Taggart about the whole idea."

"I'll bet!" Falconi snorted.

"Robert! You don't really know Chuck Fagin," Andrea exclaimed. "None of you do. He works hard for you guys, and he tries to do what's best for you."

"Sure," Falconi said. "My main problem is trying to figure out who loves me more—Fagin or Santa Claus."

"Never mind!" Andrea said. "Let's talk about what's on your mind."

"The mission," Falconi said. "I don't like it one goddamned bit."

"It's bizarre, I'll admit," Andrea said. "But Taggart made some pretty strong arguments for it. There are legions of potential agents out there in the intelligence community who would decide their loyalty on the outcome of this showdown with the Red Bears."

"Loyalty? *Loyalty!*" Falconi exclaimed. "That's

47

a poor choice of words."

"Very well," Andrea said. "Let's just say these agents will choose which side they'll serve."

"It seems more like street gangs having a rumble than doing real battle," Falconi said. He got another cigarette.

"Robert!"

"Stop bitching me out, for Chrissake!" he admonished her, lighting up. "I still have some heavy thinking to do. This situation is murky and crazy as hell."

"It's pretty clear," Andrea said. "Although no orders have been issued yet, it's only a matter of time."

Falconi took another thoughtful drag. "Everything – orders, infiltration, battle, death – it's all a matter of time."

Jean was in bed asleep, but her husband Malpractice McCorckel sat on the balcony of their apartment. Sitting beside him, and drinking a cold beer, Sgt. Maj. Top Gordon was at peace with the world.

The two had been silent for quite some time before Malpractice finally spoke. "You guys didn't fool me, you know?"

Top looked over at him. "What?"

"I said that you – Falconi and you – didn't fool me one goddamned bit," Malpractice said. "And that goes for the sly Swift Elk too."

"What're you talking about?" Top asked.

"I'm talking about that administrative leave

you sent me and Calvin Culpepper on," Malpractice said. "Falconi said it was because we'd been
on ten missions and needed a break."

"Yeah," Top said. He didn't like the direction
the conversation was drifting, so he quickly
drained the bottle. "I'm gonna get another beer.
You want one?"

"Yeah. And hurry up."

Top, feeling slightly troubled, went into the
kitchen and returned with two full bottles. "Is
something bothering you, Malpractice?"

"No," the detachment medic said. "It ain't exactly bothering me. But I want you to know that
I wasn't fooled a bit."

"You already said that. But listen up," Top
said. He wanted to end the conversation quickly
and neatly. "The old man figured you and Calvin
had some leave time coming, so he gave you each
furloughs. That was all there was to it."

"Calvin didn't need no administrative leave,"
Malpractice said. "*I* needed it. Hell, I'm a medic
and I recognized the symptoms I was showing
during the operation on the Song Cai. I was
snapping at ever'body, and giving Falconi a hard
time."

Top didn't say anything for awhile. He just
drank his beer as he tried to figure the best way
to handle the sensitive matter that Malpractice
had brought up. When he did speak, he chose his
words carefully. "Yeah. You're an old soldier,
Malpractice, so I won't bullshit you. The colonel
and I—and Swift Elk too—thought you were
riding a one way train into psychoville. We also

49

knew you were fighting like hell to stay on the up-and-up. If we offered you a furlough by yourself you wouldn't have taken it, right?"

Malpractice nodded his head. "Right."

"So, since you and Calvin had been in the deep shit together longer'n anybody else, we thought it would work out good to give both you guys a break," Top said. "And it worked."

"Yeah," Malpractice said. "I ain't arguing with that. I just said you wasn't fooling me."

"We really didn't try to."

"Maybe not," Malpractice said. His tone was serious. "I won't go near that 'bend' again, Top. I'm in complete control."

"Yeah," Top agreed. "You are."

Malpractice raised his voice. "I mean it, goddamnit, Top!"

"I believe you," Top said.

"Shit!" Malpractice said angrily.

Top reached over and patted him on the shoulder. "Look, Malpractice, you're in my team. You're my automatic rifleman, right?"

"Damned right," Malpractice said.

"That makes you my second-in-command," Top said. "If I thought you couldn't hack it no more, I sure as hell wouldn't keep you in that position. And neither would Falconi."

Malpractice knew the sergeant major was speaking the unadulterated truth. He slowly finished off his beer. Then he smiled. "I feel better, Top."

"So do I, Malpractice," Top said.

"Want another beer?"

"Damned straight," Top answered.

"I'll get it," Malpractice said.

"You'd damned well better," Top growled good-naturedly. "After all, I am your top sergeant."

"Asshole!" Malpractice growled as he headed for the kitchen. But he was grinning to himself.

"Hey!" Top called out. "You call that respectful?"

Malpractice looked back and winked. "Call it insolent friendliness."

"Just get the beer," Top said. He was glad they'd had that conversation. The air was clear as a bell now.

Chapter 4

Archie Dobbs lethargically moved the broom around the floor again. The place was already cleaned up and further sweeping on his part would do nothing to improve the appearance of the place. But after three days of lonely waiting, he was so bored that he would do anything, even useless chores, to make the time go by faster. The latrine was spotless and shining, and there wasn't as much as a single smudge on any window in the building.

The other sign of his boredom was a GI garbage can filled to the brim with empty beer cans. He'd finished off the ones that Malpractice had left him and run through two other cases besides.

A prop-driven aircraft took off in the distance and Archie stopped his make-work project to listen to it. He tried to guess what it was: A four or two engine perhaps? Transport or recon aircraft? Or perhaps one of the old-fashioned World

War II type fighters used by the South Vietnamese as effective ground support for infantry.

But before he could really become engrossed in the game, the aircraft's engine roar faded away. There was a moment of silence, then the sound of another type of motor became apparent to him. Archie strained his ears, then the noise became louder. He rushed to the window and looked out. He caught sight of what he had been frantically waiting for all those dreary days.

The detachment was returning!

He rushed outside and waited while a jeep and a two-and-a-half ton truck pulled up outside the quarters. The men in the jeep — Falconi, Top Gordon, Malpractice McCorckel and Ray Swift Elk — hopped out and strode rapidly for the building.

Archie grinned and rendered a snappy salute as they approached. The first guy was Lieutenant Swift Elk. This officer, the second-in-command of the detachment under Lieutenant Colonel Falconi, winked at Archie. "Hi, Archie. How's tricks?"

"I'm bored out of my skull," Archie said. "Glad to see you guys. Really!"

Ray Swift Elk, a full-blooded Sioux Indian was lean and muscular. His copper-colored skin, hawkish nose, and high cheek bones gave him the appearance of the classic prairie warrior. There were still dark spots on his fatigues where he'd removed his master sergeant chevrons. Brand new cloth insignia of an infantry lieutenant were sewn on his collar.

Twelve years of service in Special Forces had

made Swift Elk particularly well-qualified to be the detachment executive officer. This particular position was important because, in reality, he was Falconi's second-in-command.

In spite of his skills and education in modern soldiering, Swift Elk still considered his ancestral past an important part of his life, and he practiced Indian customs when and where able. Part of his tribe's history included some vicious combats against the Black troopers of the U.S. Cavalry's 9th and 10th Regiments of the racially segregated army of the 19th century. The Sioux warriors had nicknamed the black men they fought "Buffalo Soldiers". This was because of their hair which, to the Indians, was like the thick manes on the buffalo. The appelation was a sincere compliment due to these native Americans' veneration of the bison. Ray Swift Elk called both black guys in the detachment — Calvin Culpepper and Dwayne Simpson — "Buffalo Soldiers," and he did so with the same respect his ancestors used during the Plains Wars.

The next man to approach was Sergeant Major Gordon. As the senior non-commissioned officer of the Black Eagles, he was tasked with several pre-operational responsibilities. Besides having to take the OPLAN and use it to form the basic OPORD for the missions, he was also responsible for maintaining discipline and efficiency within the unit.

Top was a husky man, his jet-black hair thinning perceptibly, looking even more sparse because of the strict G.I. haircut he wore. His entrance into the Black Eagles had been less than satisfactory. After seventeen years spent in the army's elite spit-and-polish airborne infantry units, he had brought in an attitude that did not fit well with the diverse individuals in Falconi's command. Gordon's zeal to follow army regulations to the letter had cost him a marriage when his wife, fed up with having a husband who thought more of the army than her, filed for divorce and took their kids back to the old hometown in upstate New York. Despite that heartbreaking experience, he hadn't let up a bit. To make things worse in the Black Eagles, he had taken the place of a popular detachment sergeant who was killed in action on the Song Bo River. This noncom, called "Top" by the men, was an old Special Forces man who knew how to handle the type of soldier who volunteered for unconventional units. The new top sergeant would have been resented no matter what type of man he was.

Gordon's first day in his new assignment brought him into quick conflict with the Black Eagles personnel that soon got to far out of hand that Falconi began to seriously consider relieving the sergeant and seeing to his transfer back to a regular airborne unit.

But during Operation Laos Nightmare, Gordon's bravery under fire earned him the grudging respect of the lower-ranking Black Eagles. Finally, when he fully realized the problems he had created for himself, he changed his methods of leadership. Gordon backed off doing things by the book and found he could still maintain good discipline and efficiency while getting rid of the chicken-shit aspects of army life. It was most apparent he had been accepted by the men when they bestowed the nickname "Top" on him.

He had truly become the "top sergeant" then.

The detachment medic, SFC Malcomb "Malpractice" McCorkel, followed right on Top Gordon's heels. An inch under six feet in height, Malpractice had been in the army for twelve years. He had a friendly face and spoke softly as he pursued his duties in seeing after the illnesses and hurts of his buddies. He nagged and needled them to keep that wild bunch healthy. They bitched back at him, but not angrily, because each Black Eagle appreciated his concern. They all knew that nothing devised by puny man could keep Malpractice from reaching a wounded detachment member and pulling him back to safety. Malpractice was unique in the unit for another reason too. He was the only married man under Falconi's command.

Lt. Col. Robert Falconi himself followed Malpractice. He stopped and held out his hand to Archie. "How's it going, pal?"

"I'm doing all right, sir," Archie said. Then he added, "but I sure do miss my girl."

"You made one of the most serious and basic of military mistakes," Falconi said seriously.

"Yes, sir. I know. I missed a troop movement," Archie said.

"That was incidental," Falconi said. "The real

problem came in getting a sergeant major pissed off at you."

"I'll roger that, sir," Archie said. "But I'll make it quits between him and me. Don't you worry."

"You can console yourself with one thought," Falconi said. He jerked a thumb back at the other detachment members. "This enforced sojourn into good behavior has put you in better shape than those poor dumb bastards." He laughed and patted Archie's shoulder. "See you later."

"Yes, sir." Archie turned his attention to his buddies who moved slowly toward him. Bedraggled, obviously fatigued and suffering from numberous cuts and abrasions, the former revelers had now officially reported back to duty. But Archie was deliriously happy to see them. "Hi ya, guys!" he sang out. "Man, it's great to see you!"

The only response he got from the beaten, hung-over crowd was silence and bleary-eyed glares.

The first man to the door was the detachment's slowest, easiest going guy. PO Blue Richards was a fully-qualified Navy Seal. A red-haired Alabamian with a gawky, good-natured grin common to good ol' country boys, Blue had been named after his "daddy's favorite huntin' dawg." An expert in demolitions either on land or underwater, Blue considered himself honored for his father to have given him that dog's name.

The next man was marine Staff Sgt. Paulo

Garcia. Under the new reorganization of the detachment, Paulo performed the intelligence work for the Black Eagles. Of Portuguese descent, this former tuna fisherman from San Diego, California, had joined the marines at the relatively late age of twenty-one after deciding to look for a bit of adventure. There was always marine corps activity to see around his hometown, and he decided that fighting group offered him exactly what he was looking for. Ten years of service and plenty of combat action in the Demilitarized Zone and Khe Sanh made him more than qualified for the Black Eagles.

The unit's supply sergeant was a truly talented and enterprising staff sergeant named Enrique "Hank" Valverde. He had been in the army for ten years. Hank began his career as a supply clerk, quickly finding ways to cut through army red tape to get logistical chores taken care of quickly and efficiently. He made the rank of sergeant in the very short time of only two years, finally volunteering for the Green Berets in the late 1950s. Hank Valverde found that Special Forces was the type of unit that offered him the finest opportunity to hone and practice his legendary supply expertise.

Sgt. Dwayne Simpson, one of the two men called "Buffalo Soldier" by Swift Elk, certainly had family connections to the nickname. A black man from Arizona, his family had served in both the segregated army of the 19th and early 20th centuries, and the modern integrated service for four generations. He was a qualified ranger with a solid ten years of service to back up his expertise as a heavy weapons specialist.

A navy corpsman, Doc Robichaux was a Cajun born and bred in Louisiana. He, like Blue Richards, had a good background in the Seals. He'd spent plenty of time in the "Brown Water Navy" and had also seen combat with marine infantry units. A short, swarthy young man, he had a friendly face and could play a fiddle that would make a Louisiana Saturday night jump 'til dawn. Although assigned as a rifleman, he would be expected to help Malpractice McCorckel in the medical aspect of activities when needed.

SFC Calvin Culpepper was a tall, brawny black man who had entered the army off a poor Georgia farm his family had worked as sharecroppers. Although now a team leader in the detachment, he used to handle all the demolition chores. His favorite tool in that line of work was C4 plastic explosive. It was said he could set off a charge under a silver dollar and get back ninety-nine cents change. Resourceful, intelligent, and combatwise, Calvin, the other "Buffalo Soldier," pulled his weight—and then a bit more—in the dangerous undertakings of the Black Eagles.

The first of the newer men now made their forlorn appearances. Although Sgt. Gunnar Olson had officially taken part in one Black Eagle mission, he'd served with them before that particular event. During the operation on the Song Cai River he'd been a gunner—appropriately called Gunnar the Gunner—on a helicopter gunship that flew fire support operations for

Falconi and his men. Gunnar was so impressed with the detachment that he immediately put in for a transfer to the unit. Falconi quickly approved the paperwork and hired Gunnar the Gunner on as the unit's machine gunner. Now armed with an M60 machine gun, Gunnar, of Norwegian descent from Minnesota, looked forward to his new work assignment.

Tiny Burke, who acted as Gunnar's ammo bearer, was the lowest ranking member of the unit. He was not really qualified mentally for the Green Berets or Black Eagles, but this big, hulking guy had been Gunnar's loader in their helicopter outfit. Not real bright, he made up for his lack of brainpower with physical strength, devotion and bull-like bravery. Tiny stood six feet, four inches tall and weighed in at a muscular two hundred and twenty pounds. The ammo cans he carried looked like tin pill boxes in his huge mitts.

Another new man, Sgt. Jesse Makalue, was from Hawaii. Almost as big as Tiny, he was a great natural athlete who could have gotten himself a cushy job participating in a variety of sports at some of the larger army posts. But Jesse liked danger and both shooting and hitting people. Referee's whistles always pissed him off due to his dislike of interference to violence. He was a steady NCO, but had a vicious temper that demanded a lot of control on his part.

Jesse was trailed by navy PO 1/C Sparks Johnson. As Falconi's communications chief, he served under an ominous tradition. He was the third man for the job and, like all the others, was navy. All his predecessors—Petty Officers Fred Jackson, Durwood Martin and Leland Brewster—had not survived more than three Black Eagle missions. Falconi had fully appraised Sparks of the jinx on the job, but the Seal had only shrugged. "There ain't nobody supposed to live forever."

The US Marine Corps' latest contribution to the Black Eagles was Staff Sgt. Salty O'Rourke. This ageless wonder had over twenty-five years of service. Salty kept himself in outstanding physical condition and had been known as one of the toughest drill instructors in the corps. By rights, Salty should have been a sergeant major—or at least a gunnery sergeant—but his rather marked lack of social finesse and tendency to settle things with his fists, kept him from moving into the more elite non-commissioned officer positions in the headquarters of higher echelon units.

The final man into the billets was Sgt. Dean Fotopoulus. A Greek-American from Chicago, he'd moved from the sport of wrestling, where he'd had a college scholarship, to the martial art of karate. His devotion to this skill had earned him a black belt, and the discipline learned from it made Special Forces seem attractive. Now with seven years of service, he was looking forward to this newest phase of his military career.

The men trooped inside and immediately fell on their bunks. There were even a couple of snores until Sgt. Maj. Top Gordon had endured all he could put up with.

"On your fucking feet, you stinking drunken bastards!" he bellowed. "A week of fornicating and drunken revelry don't earn you no sacktime!"

The men stumbled awkwardly out into the center aisle and assumed swaying positions of attention. Archie Dobbs, sober and clear headed, grinned. Then he displayed a serious expression. "I'm shocked at these fellows, Sergeant Major," he said. "And I demand that you reprimand them vigorously for their disgraceful conduct."

"Shut up, Dobbs!"

"Yes, Sergeant Major!" Archie yelled out.

"Okay. Ever'body outside," Top ordered. "Five miles of double-timing in boots will clear the cobwebs out of your cloudy minds."

"P.T.?" Blue groaned.

"Right!" Top loudly replied. "And that'll include a few choice exercises from the Daily Dozen."

Doc Robichaux was shocked. "What the hell for, Top? You act like we're goin' on a mission or sumthin'."

"Yeah," Calvin Culpepper said. He glanced around. "But that couldn't be so, or else ol' Fagin would be here."

The door burst open and Chuck Fagin stepped inside displaying a wide grin.

"You called?"

Chapter 5

Seventeen pairs of boots struck the pavement on the outer runway of Peterson Field as the Black Eagles, under Sgt. Maj. Top Gordon's stern command, pounded away on their P.T. run. The group was dressed in T-shirts, fatigue trousers and boots while performing this physically taxing task under the blistering tropical sun.

Top was in charge of this formation, and even Lieutenant Colonel Falconi and First Lieutenant Swift Elk heeded his orders. They also lustily replied to his chanting as he took the detachment through its paces.

"Black Eagles! Black Eagles! All the way! This is the way we start our day!"

Their lungs were worked doubly by the demands of running in step as well as having to keep up the orchestrated shouting.

Under these awesome conditions, the Black Eagles ran on.

"G.I. Beans and G. I. Gravy!
Gee I wished I'd joined the navy!"

Blue took exception to the last chorus. "Hey!" he yelled out. "I *did* join the navy!"

Top, offended by this break in proper protocol, whipped his head around and pointed straight at the Navy Seal. "Drop out for twenty push-ups, Blue!"

"Aye, aye, Sergeant Major," Blue said. He dutifully jumped from the formation and began to immediately perform the required number of punishment repetitions of the exercise.

Blue, the sweat now really starting to stream down his face, looked up from the front-leaning rest position while the Black Eagles ran on.

"If I die on the ol' drop zone,
Box me up and ship me home.
Pin my wings upon my chest,
Tell my girl I did my best!"

Archie Dobbs was having a hell of a good time. Fresh and eager, he sailed along feeling great. But his pals, sweating out the booze and the late nights, labored through the physical torture that the merciless Top demanded of them.

It was one hundred per cent sweat and strain as the Black Eagles ran on.

64

"Black Eagles, Black Eagles have you
heard?
I'm gonna jump from the Big Iron Bird.
And if my 'chute don't open wide,
I'll be splattered over the countryside!"

Falconi and Swift Elk at the head of the double column kept the pace steady and true. Side-
by-side, they flashed grins of encouragement at
each other despite the growing burn of fatigue in
their laboring legs.

"Wine! Women! Wine! Women!
No good! No good!
I gotta go Black Eagles, Black Eagles,
All the way! All the way!"

Tiny Burke's long legs aided him in keeping
up, but his heavy bodyweight—despite the fact
it was nearly all muscle—took its toll too. The
big man winced against the pain, trying to ignore it and let the chanting raise his morale.

"There ain't no use in looking down.
There ain't no discharge on the ground!
Am I right or wrong?"

"You're right!" the detachment responded to
Top's question.
"Tell me if I'm wrong," Top urged them.
"You're right!" the suffering men assured the
sergeant major.

Meanwhile, Blue had finished his twenty push-ups and leaped back to his feet. He had to run like hell to catch up with his buddies. When he did, he fell in on the rear of the formation.

"There ain't no use in going home,
Jody's got your gal and gone!"

With that bit of morale-raising news that their girl friends back in the States were probably two-timing them with some cruddy civilian, the detachment turned off the runway and continued their syncopated torture across the grassy area that led to their quarters. There were audible sighs of relief when they arrived and Top took them off the double-time routine.

"Quick-time," Top ordered. "March!"

They immediately fell into the slower quick-time pace and marched on. Now that the chanting had ceased, their heavy panting was clearly audible.

"Hut, two, thu-rep, foah! Hut, two, thu-rep, foah!" Top yelled out, counting the cadence as they arrived in front of their billets. "De-tachment, halt!"

There was a crash of boots as they came to a stomping halt. Top looked at them and smiled. "Right, face!"

Now thoroughly winded, they waited with numb impatience for the command to dismiss them.

But Top was far from finished with them. "Oh, my! Oh, my! Are you tired?" the sergeant major asked.

The detachment, panting and sweating, glanced up at him. Blue spoke their collective minds for them. "Top," he said. "We been rode hard and put away wet."

"Poor babies," Top clucked. "I'm pooped myself." Then he grinned wickedly. "Open ranks, march! Half right, face! Front leaning rest, move!"

Paulo Garcia winced. "Oh, no, no, no, no!"

"Now that we've had our little run," Top announced. "We'll rest up by doing some nice soothing push-ups. On my count, you drunken bastards! Ready, exercise! One! Two! Three! Four! One! Two! —"

They didn't stop at push-ups. Following this shoulder-numbing movement, they went on to squat-jumpers, bend-and-reaches, squat-thrusts, turn-and-bounces, then more push-ups. After a hectic twenty minute pace, Top got them on their feet again. "Half left, face! Close ranks, march! Okay, I gave you a break from running. Let's get back to work. Right, face! Forward, march! Double-time, march!"

Once again there was the coordinated pounding of boot leather on concrete as the Black Eagles moved out sharply.

"Lift your heads and hold 'em high!
The Black Eagle men are passing by!
Black Eagles, Black Eagles all the way!

This is the way we start our day!
Am I right or wrong?"
"You're right!"
"Tell me if I'm wrong!"
"You're right!"

They made two more complete circuits of Peterson Field. The ARVN security unit, keeping out of the heat under the shade of the corrugated-iron roofs over their gun positions, watched the toiling men with genuine sympathy. It was like the old saying: "Only mad dogs and Englishmen go out in the mid-day sun."

Well, the Black Eagles do more than just go out in it, they *run* like hell in the blazing rays.

But finally, even Sgt. Maj. Top Gordon showed some mercy, and they were trooped back to their quarters. This time, after a token gesture of only fifty push-ups, they were finally dismissed to stagger inside to the showers.

Chuck Fagin and Andrea Thuy stood by the door giving them well-deserved applause as the men went into the billets. Then the two went into the dayroom at the other side of the building to await them.

A half hour later, washed down and relatively refreshed, they appeared in the dayroom. Archie went over to the big cooler and flipped it open. Then he stepped back in shock and dismay.

"There ain't no beer in there!"

Eyes watered as mouths were opened in silent screams of horror. Salty O'Rourke of the Marine Corps was the first to recover. He limped over to

Fagin and grabbed him by the collar. "Where's the goddamned beer?"

Fagin had trouble talking with his throat restricted, but he managed to squeak out the words, "Falconi – says – no – beer."

"Oh, shit!" Salty said. He released the CIA man, and turned to the others. "Maybe we better wait for the colonel, guys."

All agreed it was a good idea. They quickly helped themselves to the soft drinks in the cooler and settled down on the sofas and chairs in the dayroom.

A couple of minutes later, Lieutenant Colonel Falconi, trailed by Lieutenant Swift Elk and Sergeant Major Gordon came in. Falconi nodded to them. "I suppose you noticed there wasn't any beer."

Malpractice McCorckel, feigning surprise, stood up and looked into the cooler. "Why, for heaven's sake! There isn't any, is there?"

"Gee!" Calvin Culpepper exclaimed in a falsetto voice. "To tell you the truth, I really hadn't given it much thought one way or the other."

"Knock it off, wise-asses," Falconi said. "I did this on purpose to keep you dried out."

"Right," Archie Dobbs said raising a can of Coke. "For the next mission, right?"

"Right," Falconi said. "But this next operation is going to be entirely different from any others we've been on."

"What's so unusual?" Sparks Johnson asked. "Does this one have some real planning behind it?"

"No," Falconi answered. "That isn't what makes it unique. The strange thing about this one is that it's voluntary – I say again – *voluntary!*"

There was a stunned silence until Blue Richards slowly shook his head in wonderment. "Voluntary?"

"And that's not all," Falconi said. He fished in his jacket pocket and pulled out a single sheet of paper. "Here's the Operation Order. And that's all we'll get."

Paulo Garcia belched some Pepsi. "You mean Fagin ain't gonna load us down with paperwork this time?"

Falconi raised his hands in a signal that indicated he didn't want any bullshit. "It's this way, guys. We have some counterparts on the other side of the Iron Curtain. They're a bunch of commie goons called the Red Bears. There are seventeen of them – just like us – and they're in Southeast Asia."

"Great!" Dwayne Simpson said. "Let's find the bastards and kick their asses, sir."

"That's exactly what they want us to do," Falconi said. "An operational area has been chosen between South and North Vietnam. We're going in with only what we can carry on our backs. The Red Bears will be doing the same thing. No re-supply and no medevac," Falconi said. Then he added, " – and no mercy."

Doc Robichaux lit a cigarette. "This sounds like an orchestrated contest," he remarked.

"That's exactly what it is," Falconi said. "And we're going to be watched closely by the world's intelligence community. The winner of this campaign is going to be impressive as hell. It should win over double-agents and other despicable bastards who will feel safer dealing for our side rather than working for the losers' bosses."

Ray Swift Elk, who had already been fully briefed, made a contribution to the briefing. "You guys know my intelligence background. Just let me tell you that this is important. It will affect the cloak-and-dagger business all over this beat-up old planet we live on. That includes NATO, Africa, Asia, Latin America, or wherever else we're trying to conduct clandestine operations for the Free World."

Jessie Makalue, the Hawaiian, was more pragmatic. "What about cheating, huh?"

Fagin now joined the discussion. "There won't be any. Observers will not be impressed with hanky-panky from either side. You wade in there and duke it out. If you run out of ammo, you'll go with knives and bayonets. After that, you'll go hand-to-hand." Then he scowled. "Or you'll quit."

Blue Richards' Alabama drawl was cold. "No way, Fagin. We'll die, maybe. But we won't quit."

"I can guarantee you that the Red Bears won't quit either," Fagin said. "Their leader is a KGB sonofabitch named Krashchenko. He's got a personal score to settle with you guys. He's spent a couple of years directing efforts against you. Remember those East Germans that infiltrated into South Vietnam in American uniforms? Or those fucking Algerians not too long ago? They

71

were Krashchenko's guys. And now he's coming in person with just one thing on his mind — killing you guys."

"The Russki motherfucker better bring company," Archie Dobbs said.

"He's bringing in sixteen hard-cases with him," Fagin said. "Bulgarian mountain troopers, Russian paratroopers and naval infantry, Polish border guards and more East Germans."

Sergeant Major Gordon, not an easy man to impress, lit a cigar. "This is going to be the toughest bunch we've ever faced."

Archie forced a laugh. "So? They'll take a little longer to kill, that's all."

"Yeah," Calvin Culpepper echoed. "Communist mothers will be proud to have their sons killed by Black Eagles."

There were some approving cheers, but Falconi remained somber. "I like confidence," he said. "However, I hate over-confidence. There is one fact I want you to keep in the forefront of your thoughts as we go through this god-awful showdown we're facing."

"Give us the word, sir!" Malpractice McCorckel urged him.

"All the guys who go into this mission won't be coming out," Falconi said. "We've been ignoring what I brought up before. So I say again: This is purely voluntary. For the first time, we will excuse you if you feel this is useless or foolhardy. Because, goddamnit, it sure as hell is."

Nobody spoke and nobody moved. Their silence shouted the dedication of the Black Eagles.

Andrea Thuy, who had been silently standing in the back of the room by the door, suddenly slipped outside. When she was by herself, she wiped at tears that streamed down her face. "God!" she said in a weak voice as emotion overcame her. "God—oh, sweet God!"

Deep in her heart she knew she was seeing history being written before her eyes. But it would never be in school books or shown for later generations on television specials. No movies, no stories or any other type of media would play out this story. The situation, being so calmly discussed by the men inside, was Valley Forge, the Alamo and Pork Chop Hill all wrapped into one.

Andrea worked to recover her emotions and steel herself to go back into the room. Another thing she realized was that she was also seeing some of her best, dearest friends for the last time. Perhaps even Robert Falconi, the man she loved.

Now dry-eyed and calm, Andrea slipped back inside to continue listening to Falconi's briefing. Archie Dobbs noticed her. He turned to Andrea and winked.

She smiled and nodded to him, giving the "thumbs-up" signal.

But the previous words spoken ran through her mind:

Dwayne Simpson: *Let's find the bastards and kick their asses!*

Blue Richards: *We'll die maybe. But we won't quit!*

73

Calvin Culpepper: *Communist mothers will be proud to have their sons killed by Black Eagles!*

Robert Falconi: *All the guys who go into this mission won't be coming out!*

Andrea forced another smile then settled down to listen to Falconi's full briefing.

Chapter 6

The Black Eagles did not suddenly spring into being. On the other hand, they were not a slowly evolving old established unit with years of tradition behind them either.

In reality, they were the brainchild of a Central Intelligence Agency case officer named Clayton Andrews. But his creation of the detachment was not an easy process by any means. His initial plans to activate the unit were met with the usual stodgy, stupid resistance that military bureaucrats—like all bureaucrats—give to any innovative new ideas. But Clayton Andrews was not the kind of individual to take such mindless rebuffs kindly.

That man growled and kicked through knotted red tape for months before he finally received the official okay to turn his concept of creating an independent band of jungle fighters into a living, breathing, ass-kicking reality.

In those early days of the 1960s, "Think Tanks" of PhDs at various centers of American political thought and study were conducting mental wrestling matches with the question of fighting Communism in southeast Asia. The threat of this ideology spreading in that part of the world was very real indeed, and some of the best brains in the country were assigned to come up with a solution for containing this political and military force.

Andrews was involved in that same program, but in a tremendously more physical way than the brainy types. The work he did was not intellectual, it was purely physical.

He was in combat.

And the CIA man participated in more than just a small amount of clandestine fighting in Cambodia, Laos, and Vietnam. He hit it in a big way, which included a hell of a lot of missions that went beyond mere harassment operations in Viet Cong and Pathet Lao areas. His main job was the conduct of penetrations into North Vietnam itself. Over a very short period of time this dangerous assignment cost plenty of good men their lives because some of the personnel involved, no matter how dedicated or brave, were not the proper men for such a dangerous undertaking. The appalling casualty rate motivated Andrews to begin his battle with the stodgy military administration to set things up properly.

It took diplomatic persuasion – combined with a few ferocious outbreaks of temper – before the program was eventually expanded. When the final approval was granted, Andrews was suddenly thrust into a position where he needed not simply an *excellent* combat commander, he needed the *best*. Thus, he began an extensive search for an officer to lead that special detachment he needed to carry out certain down-and-dirty missions.

There were months of personnel investigations and countless interviews with hopeful contenders for the job. In the end, after his exhaustive effort, Andrews settled on a Special Forces captain named Robert Falconi.

Pulling all the strings he had, Andrews saw to it that the Green Beret officer was transferred to his own branch of SOG – the Special Operations Group – to begin work on this brand new project.

Captain Falconi was tasked with organizing a new fighting unit to be known as the Black Eagles. This group's basic policy was to be primitive and simple, and Falconi summed it up in his own words: "Seek out the enemy and kill the sons of bitches."

Their mission was to penetrate deep into the heartland of the communists to disrupt, destroy, maim and slay. The men who would belong to the Black Eagles would be volunteers from every branch of the armed forces. And that was to include all nationalities involved in the struggle against the Red invasion of South Vietnam.

Each man was to be an absolute master in his particular brand of military mayhem. He had to be an expert in not only his own nation's firearms but also those of other friendly and enemy countries. But the required knowledge in weaponry didn't stop at the modern types. This also included knives, bludgeons, garrotes, and even crossbows when the need to deal silent death had arisen.

There was also a requirement for the more sophisticated and peaceful vocations too. Foreign languages, land navigation, communications, medical skills and even mountaineering and scuba diving were to be within the realm of knowledge of the Black Eagles. Then, in addition, each man was to know how to type. In an outfit that had no clerks, this office skill was extremely important because each man had to do his own paperwork. Much of this was operations orders that directed their highly complicated, dangerous missions. These documents had to be legible and easy to read in order to avoid confusing, deadly errors in combat.

Now it was Falconi who combed through 201-files and called up men for interviews. Some he had served with before, others he knew by reputation, while there were also hundreds whose military records reflected their qualifications. Scores were interviewed, but in the end only a dozen were selected.

They became the enforcement arm of SOG, drawing the missions which were the most dangerous and sensitive. In essence they were hit men, closely coordinated and completely dedicated, held together and directed through the forceful personality of their leader Capt. Robert Falconi.

After Clayton Andrews was promoted out of the job, a new CIA officer moved in. This was Chuck Fagin. An ex-paratrooper and veteran of both World War II and the Korean War, Fagin had a natural talent when it came to dreaming up nasty things to do to the unfriendlies up north. It didn't take him long to get Falconi and his boys busy.

Their first efforts were directed against a pleasure palace in North Vietnam.[1] This bordello *par excellence* was used by communist officials during their retreats from the trials and tribulations of administering authority and regulation over their slave populations. There were no excesses, perverted tastes or unusual demands that went unsatisfied in this hidden fleshpot.

Falconi and his wrecking crew sky-dived into the operational area in a HALO (High Altitude Low Opening) infiltration, and when the Black Eagles finished their raid on the whorehouse, there was hardly a soul left alive to continue the debauchery.

Their next hell-trek into the enemy's hinterlands was an even more dangerous assignment with the difficulty factor multiplied by the special demands placed on them.[2] The North Vietnamese had set up a special prison camp in which they were perfecting their skills in the torture-interrogation of downed American pilots. With the conflict escalating in Southeast Asia, they rightly predicted they would soon have more than just a few Yanks in their hands. A North Korean brainwashing expert had come

[1] Black Eagles No. 1 — *Hanoi Hellground*

[2] Black Eagles No. 2 — *Mekong Massacre*

over from his native country to teach them the fine points of mental torment. He had learned his despicable trade during the Korean War when he had American POWs directly under his control. His use of psychological torture, combined with just the right amount of physical torment, had broken more than one man despite the most spirited resistance. Experts who studied his methods came to the conclusion that only a completely insane prisoner, whose craziness caused him to abandon both the sensation of pain and the instinct for survival, could have resisted the North Korean's methods.

At the time of the Black Eagles' infiltration into North Vietnam, the prisoners behind the barbed wire were few – but important. A USAF pilot, an army Special Forces sergeant, and two high-ranking officers of the South Vietnamese forces were the unwilling tenants of the concentration camp.

Falconi and his men were not only tasked to rescue the POWs but also had to bring along the prison's commandant and his North Korean tutor. Falconi pulled off the job, fighting his way south through the North Vietnamese army and air force to a bloody showdown on the Song Bo River. The situation deteriorated to the point that the Black Eagles' magazines had their last few rounds in them as they waited for the NVA's final charge. But the unexpected but spirited aid from anti-communist guerrillas turned the tide, and the Black Eagles smashed their way out of the encirclement.

The next operation took them to Laos where they were pitted against the fanatical savages of the Pathet Lao.[3] If that wasn't bad enough, their method of entrance into the operational area was bizarre and dangerous. This type of transport into battle hadn't been used in active combat in more than twenty years. It had even been labeled obsolete by military experts. But this didn't deter the Black Eagles from the idea.

They used a glider to make a silent flight to a secret landing zone. If that wasn't bad enough, the operations plan called for their extraction through a glider-recovery apparatus that not only hadn't been tested in combat, but had never been given sufficient trial under rehearsed, safe conditions.

After a hairy ride in the flimsy craft, they hit the ground to carry out a mission designed to destroy the construction site of a Soviet nuclear power plant the Reds wanted to install in the area. Everything went wrong from the start, and the Black Eagles fought against a horde of insane zealots until their extraction to safety. This was completely dependent on the illegal and unauthorized efforts of a dedicated USAF pilot — the same one they had rescued from the North Vietnam prison camp. The air force colonel was determined to help the same men who had saved him, and he came through with all pistons firing, paying the debt he owed Falconi's guys.

This hairy episode was followed by two occur-

[3] Black Eagles No. 3 — *Nightmare in Laos*

rences: The first was Capt. Robert Falconi's promotion to major, and the second was a mission that had been doubly dangerous because of an impossibility to make firm operation plans. Unknown Caucasian personnel, posing as US troops, had been committing atrocities against Vietnamese peasants.[4] The situation had gotten far enough out of control that the effectiveness of American efforts in the area had been badly damaged. Once again Falconi and the Black Eagles were called in to put things right. They went in on a dark beach from a submarine and began a determined reconnaissance until they finally made contact with their quarry.

These enemy agents, wearing US army uniforms, were dedicated East German communists prepared to fight to the death for their cause. The Black Eagles admired such unselfish dedication to the extent that they gave the Reds the opportunity to accomplish that end: Sacrifice their lives for communism.

But this wasn't successfully concluded without the situation deteriorating to the point the Black Eagles had to endure human wave assaults from a North Vietnamese army battalion led by an infuriated general. This officer had been humiliated by Falconi on the Song Bo River several months previously. The mission ended in another Black Eagles victory, but not before five more good men had died.

Brought back to Saigon at last, the seven

[4] Black Eagles No. 4—*Pungi Patrol*

survivors of the previous operations cleaned their weapons, drew fresh, clean uniforms and prepared for a long awaited period of R&R – Rest and Recreation.

It was not to be.

Chuck Fagin's instincts and organization of agents had ferreted out information that showed a high-ranking intelligence officer of the South Vietnamese army had been leaking information on the Black Eagles to his superiors up in the Communist north.[5] It would have been easy enough to arrest this double agent, but an entire enemy espionage net had been involved. Thus, Falconi and his Black Eagles had to come in from the boondocks and fight the good fight against these spies and assassins in the back streets of Saigon itself.

When Saigon was relatively cleaned up, the Black Eagles drew a mission that involved going out on the Ho Chi Minh trail on which the North Vietnamese sent supplies, weapons and munitions south to be used by the Viet Cong and elements of the North Vietnamese army.[6] The enemy was enjoying great success despite repeated aerial attacks by the US and South Vietnamese air forces. The high command decided that only a sustained campaign conducted on the ground would put a crimp in the Reds' operation.

Naturally, they chose the Black Eagles for the

[5] Black Eagles No. 5 – *Saigon Slaughter*

[6] Black Eagles No. 6 – *AK47 Firefight*

dirty job.

Falconi and his men waged partisan warfare in its most primitive and violent fashion with raids, ambushes, and other forms of jungle fighting. The order of the day was "kill or be killed" as the monsoon forest thundered with reports of numerous types of modern weaponry. This dangerous situation was made even more deadly by a decidedly insidious and deadly form of mine warfare which made each track and trail through the brush a potential zone of death.

When this was wrapped up, Falconi and his troops received an even bigger assignment. This next operation involved working with Chinese mercenaries to secure an entire province ablaze with infiltration and invasion by the North Vietnamese army.[7] This even involved beautiful Andrea Thuy, a lieutenant in the South Vietnamese army who had been attacked to the Black Eagles. Playing on the mercenaries' superstitions and religion, she became a "warrior-sister" leading some of the blazing combat herself.

An affair of honor followed this mission, when Red agents kidnapped this lovely woman.[8] They took her north—but not for long. Falconi and the others pulled a parachute-borne attack and brought her out of the hellhole where her communist tormentors had put her.

The ninth mission, pulled off with most of the

[7] Black Eagles No. 7—*Beyond the DMZ*

[8] Black Eagles No. 8—*Boocoo Death*

detachment's veterans away on R&R involved a full-blown attack by North Vietnamese regulars into the II Corps area—all this while saddled with a pushy newspaper reporter.[9]

By that time South Vietnam had rallied quite a number of allies to her side. Besides the United States, there was South Korea, Australia, New Zealand, the Philippines, and Thailand. This situation upset the communist side and they decided to counter it by openly having various Red countries send contingents of troops to bolster the NVA (North Vietnamese Army) and the Viet Cong.

This resulted in a highly secret situation—ironically well-known by both the American and communist sides—which developed in the borderland between Cambodia and South Vietnam.[10] The Reds, in an effort to make their war against the Americans a truly international struggle, began an experimental operation involving volunteers from Algeria. These young Arab communists, led by hardcore Red officers, were to be tested against US troops. If they proved effective, other nationalities would be brought in from behind the Iron Curtain to expand the insurgency against the Americans, South Vietnamese and their allies.

Because of the possibility of failure, the Reds did not want to publicize these "volunteers" to the conflict unless the experiment proved a rousing success. The American brass also did not want the

[9] Black Eagles No. 9—*Bad Scene at Bong Son*

[10] Black Eagles No. 10—*Cambodia Kill Zone*

situation publicized under any circumstances. To do so would be to play into the world opinion manipulations of the communists.

But the generals in Saigon wanted the situation neutralized as quickly as possible.

Thus, Falconi and the Black Eagles moved into the jungle to take on the Algerians led by fanatical Major Omar Ahmed. Ahmed, who rebelled against France in Algeria, had actually fought in the French army in Indo-China as an enemy of the very people he ended up serving. Captured before the Battle of Dien Bien Phu, he had been an easy and pliable subject for the Red brainwashers and interrogators. When he returned to his native Algeria after repatriation, he was a dedicated communist ready to take on anything the free world could throw at him.

Falconi and his men, with their communication system destroyed by deceit, fought hard. But they were badly outnumbered and finally forced into a situation where their backs were literally pinned against the wall of a jungle cliff. But Archie Dobbs, injured on the infiltration jump and evacuated from the mission back to the US Army hospital at Long Binh, went AWOL in order to rejoin his buddies in combat. He not only successfully returned to them, but arrived in a helicopter gunship that threw in the fire support necessary to turn the situation around.

The communist experiment was swept away in the volleys of aerial fire and the final bayonet charge of the Black Eagles. The end result was a promotion to lieutenant colonel for Robert Falconi while his senior non-coms also were given a boost up the army's career ladder. Only Archie Dobbs, who had gone AWOL from the hospital, was demoted.

After Operation Cambodian Challenge, the Black Eagles only received the briefest of rests back at their base garrison. This return to Camp Nui Dep with fond hopes of R&R dancing through their combat-buzzed minds was interrupted by the next challenge to their courage and ingenuity. This was a mission that was dubbed Operation Song Cai Duel.[11]

Communist patrol boats had infiltrated the Song Cai River and controlled that waterway north of Dak Bla. Their activities ranged from actual raiding of river villages and military outposts, to active operations involving the transportation and infiltration of Red agents.

This campaign resulted in the very disturbing fact that the Song Cai River, though in South Vietnam, was under the complete control of Ho Chi Minh's fighters. They virtually owned the waterway.

The brass' orders to Falconi were simple: *Get the river back!*

The mission, however, was much more complicated. Distances were long, while logistics and personnel were not in the quantities needed. But that never stopped the Black Eagles before.

There were new lessons to be learned too. River navigation, powerboating and amphibious warfare

[11] Black Eagles No. 11—*Duel On the Song Cai*

had to be added to the Black Eagles' skills in jungle fighting.

Outgunned and outnumbered, Falconi and his guys waded in over their heads. The pressure mounted to the point that the village they used as a base headquarters had to be evacuated. But a surprise appearance by Chuck Fagin with a couple of quad-fifty machine guns turned the tide.

The final showdown was a gunboat battle that turned the muddy waters of the Song Cai red with blood.

It was pure hell for the men, but it was another brick laid in the wall of their brief and glorious history.

The next Black Eagle adventure began on a strange note. A French intelligence officer, who was a veteran of France's Indo-Chinese War, was attached to SOG in an advisory role. While visiting the communications room, he was invited to listen in on an intermittent radio transmission in the French language that the section had been monitoring for several months. When he heard it, the Frenchman was astounded. The broadcast was from a French soldier who correctly identified himself through code as a member of the GMI (*Groupement Mixte d'Intervention*) which had been carrying on guerrilla warfare utilizing native volunteers in the old days.[12]

Contact was made, and it was learned that this Frenchman was indeed a GMI veteran who had been reported missing-in-action during mountain

[12] Black Eagles No. 12—*Lord of Laos*

insurgency operations in 1953. And he'd done more than just survive for fifteen years. He was the leader of a large group of Meo tribesmen who were actively raiding into North Vietnam from Laos.

The information was kicked "upstairs" and the brass hats became excited. Not only was this man a proven ass-kicker, but he could provide valuable intelligence and an effective base of operations to launch further missions into the homeland of the Reds. It was officially decided to make contact with the man and bring him into the "Big Picture" by supplying him with arms, equipment and money to continue his war against the communists. The G3 Section also thought it would be a great idea to send in a detachment of troops to work with him.

They chose Lieutenant Colonel Falconi and his Black Eagles for the job.

But when the detachment infiltrated the operational area they did not find a dedicated anti-communist. Instead, they were faced with an insane French army sergeant named Farouche who regined over an opium empire high in the Laotian mountains. He had contacted the allies only for added weaponry and money in his crazy plans to wrest power from other warlords.

The mission dissolved into sheer hell. Falconi and the guys not only had to travel by foot back through five hundred miles of enemy territory to reach the safety of friendly lines, but they had to fight both the communists and Farouche's tribesmen every step of the way.

The effort cost them three good men, and when

they finally returned to safety, Archie Dobbs found that his nurse sweetheart had left him for another man. Enraged and broken-hearted, the detachment scout took off on another escapade of AWOL. This time to track down his lady love and her new boyfriend.

Falconi also expanded his Table of Organization and built up another fire team to give the detachment a grand total of three. Ray Swift Elk was commissioned an officer and made second-in-command, Sergeant Major Gordon was released from the hospital, and Malpractice McCorckel and Calvin Culpepper returned from furlough. Six new men were added to the roster so, despite Archie Dobbs' disappearance, the detachment was in damned good shape numerically.

But they didn't have long to sit back and enjoy their condition. Their next adventure came on them hard and fast after the Soviet Union had constructed a high-powered communications center in North Vietnam with the capability of monitoring and jamming satellite transmissions.[13] The project had been so secretive that it was a long while before western intelligence heard about it. Its location was hazardous for potential attackers. There were several strong military posts in the vicinity, and the area had a heavy concentration of population.

Like they said at SOG headquarters: "Only madmen or the Black Eagles would attempt to destroy the site."

---

[13] Black Eagles No. 13—*Encore At Dien Bien Phu*

Falconi was charged with infiltrating the area, blowing up the target, then getting the hell out of there. The latter part was a big problem, and the colonel came up with a bizarre exfiltration scheme. He planned to add insult to injury by meeting an aircraft on the reconstructed air strip at Dien Bien Phu that had been re-built as a tourist site.

The Black Eagles had an asset who met them on their initial entry into the operational area. This person was born and raised in the area and knew every nook and cranny of the terrain. The agent's identity was kept secret until the last possible moment, and Falconi's usual calm demeanor was sorely tested when he found himself working with Andrea Thuy—his former sweetheart from the detachment's "old days."

But despite emotional and tactical problems, Falconi directed a successful mission. The huge communications complex was blown to hell, and the aircraft was met for the escape after a few hectic hours of evading enemy troops.

It is to the Black Eagles' credit that unit integrity and morale always seemed to increase despite the staggering losses they suffered. Not long after their initial inception, the detachment decided they wanted an insignia all their own. This wasn't at all unusual for units in Vietnam. Local manufacturers, acting on designs submitted to them by the troops involved, produced these emblems that were worn by the outfits while "in country." These adornments were strictly nonregulation and unauthorized for display outside of Vietnam.

Falconi's men came up with a unique beret

badge manufactured as a cloth insignia. A larger version was used as a shoulder patch. The design consisted of a black eagle – naturally – with spread wings. The big bird's beak was opened in a defiant battle cry, and he clutched a sword in one claw and a bolt of lightning in the other. Mounted on a khaki shield that was trimmed in black, the device was an accurate portrayal of its wearers: somber and deadly.

The Black Eagles, because of the secret nature of their existence, were not always able to sport the insignia. But when they could the men wore it with great pride.

There was one more touch of their individuality that they kept to themselves. It was a motto which not only worked as a damned good password in hairy situations, but also described the Black Eagles' basic philosophy.

Those special words, in Latin, were:

CALCITRA CLUNIS!

This phrase, in the language of the ancient Romans, translated as: KICK ASS!

Chapter 7

The Red Bears, now fully acclimated to the steamy Vietnamese weather, marched into the thatched, open-air hutch that served them as a combination briefing room, mess hall and day-room.

These facilities were located at a secret military post a few kilometers west of Hanoi. The North Vietnamese Army normally used the place as a staging area for the clandestine missions destined for South Vietnam. But now, all personnel had been sent away so that only Krashchenko's detachment occupied the site hidden away in the jungle.

For average troops, the ordeal of adapting to this new environment would have been a tough one. But for the Red Bears, this was accomplished fast. Part of the selection process for this fanatical unit had been stiff psychological testing. This included both endurance and attitude toward pain. These men did not feel physical discomfort in the manner of normal people. They realized a problem was there, but somehow their minds were able to block the messages of acute suffering while continuing on with whatever activity was causing the distress. The long runs and other exercises in the high humidity and temperatures were something they were able to do while run-of-the-mill soldiers would have collapsed in heat exhaustion or utter bodily misery.

Lieutenant Colonel Krashchenko had positioned himself by the front steps of the building as the Red Bears filed in. Standing beside him, as grim as the commander, was his executive officer. This was a Russian paratroop major named Pavel Karlov. Karlov also commanded the Second Section.

Each of these sections, with the exception of the one directly under Krashchenko, was made up of the section leader and three men. All were armed with AK-47s. That one special unit to this organization was Krashchenko's First Section which consisted of a two-man heavy weapons team that served a Soviet RPD 7.62 millimeter machine gun, a rifleman for security, and the Red Bears' scout.

Karlov's Second Section was already in the hutch when the Third Section, under the command of a Bulgarian captain of mountain infantry named Todor Dzhurov, filed silently in and took their proper places on the benches along the side of the crude building. The Fourth Section came in directly behind them and followed suit as they wordlessly situated themselves. This particular unit was commanded by an East German paratrooper senior lieutenant named Eugen Deintz.

The final section to troop in was Krashchenko's. The first two men made up the machine gun team. They were a couple of Russian naval infantrymen named Ryzhyko and Grolevski. Their rifleman was a disagreeable Polish paratrooper who went by the name of Spichalski. The final man of this section was an enigmatic member of the Soviet KGB border guards. This was the scout named Ali Khail. The man was a short, incredibly muscled individual who, like the others, kept his head shaved bald. The difference in his physical appearance was an enormous handle-bar moustache. He maintained this facial adornment in a special way, keeping it carefully waxed and turned up at the ends.

Ali Khail, a Cossack, had been raised a Moslem in his native area of Azerbaijan. But he'd found the tenets of communism more attractive than those of the Koran. He took to the state with zeal after his induction into the Soviet army. A natural bully, he soon earned the stripes of sergeant on his epaulets and administered his authority with his fists and boots. This tendency toward torment brought about his initial recruitment into the KGB where further training revealed more in-born talents that he possessed: tracking and man-hunting. These latter attributes, natural skills for a Cossack, guaranteed him a place in the KGB's notorious border guard where he spent his time chasing down potential escapees from the Soviet Union's workers and peasants paradise.

Of all the men in his command, Krashchenko valued Ali Khail most, and for good reason. The colonel had worked hand-in-hand with the scout on numerous operations along the long stretches of Russia's international borders.

Now, with everyone present, Krashchenko and Karlov joined their men inside. Karlov sat down with his section while the lieutenant colonel went to the front of the room where a map board was located. "Comrades, in twenty-four hours we enter the operational area to begin what we call Operation Vengeance."

Karlov dutifully stood up and led three orchestrated cheers, then sat down once again.

Krashchenko now referred to the map. "This is the territory in which we will destroy Falconi and his Black Eagles," he said indicating the place with a pointer. "It is located so as to split exactly the line between the great people's republic of North Vietnam and the illegal, imperialist-dominated pile of shit called South Vietnam by capitalist Americans and their native puppets. The terrain there is a jungle classified as being of the monsoon variety. This means there is more undergrowth here than can be found in a tropical rain forest. Therefore, noise discipline is a must during movement through this dense vegetation."

Ali Khail, the scout, stroked his enormous moustache. "There is a border indicated in grease pencil, Comrade Lieutenant Colonel. Is that the limit of the operational area?"

"Yes," Krashchenko answered. "And I must emphasize that we are to stay within that boundary. To go beyond it, even in the noble cause of winning this great battle for world socialism, will bring harsh punishment down on us."

The East German Deintz was an instinctive cheater. He didn't like the limitations. "But, Comrade Lieutenant Colonel!" he protested. "Why not take certain advantages if they occur? Surely our glorious leaders will understand such actions on our part, *nein*—er, I mean *nyet?*"

Krashchenko was a bit impatient. "That has already been explained to you, Comrade Senior Lieutenant Deintz. This meeting in combat is being closely monitored. It is of the utmost importance that our victory be gained strictly by the rules of this particular game."

The Bulgarian Dzhurov raised his hand. "How does our weaponry compare with the Black Eagle gangsters, Comrade Lieutenant Colonel?"

"Although we have Soviet arms and they have American," Krashchenko said, "they are comparable and the same in number. We have fifteen AK47 rifles to their fifteen M16 rifles. They will employ an American M60 machine gun and we will have a Russian RPD to counteract it. Also, each man will take in four hand grenades."

That last statement brought a question from Karlov. "Are we permitted rifle grenades?"

Krashchenko shook his head. "*Nyet*—no. And allow me to inform you that ours will be the standard RG42 that will throw fragments out to approximately twenty meters. Falconi's bandits will employ the American M33. It also dispenses fragments—" Krashchenko chuckled. "—but at fifteen meters. So we have a five meter advantage there, eh, comrades!"

Ali Khail, who preferred dealing silent death with his knife, had grown tired of hearing the rules of the game. "How do we enter the operational area, *Tovarisch Podpolkovnik?*"

"We will perform a static line parachute jump here," Krashchenko said indicating an open area on the map. He moved the pointer to a similar spot farther south. "Here is where Falconi and his men will land."

Ali Khail studied the spot carefully. "We should have our first meeting with the Americans within forty-eight hours of the infiltration."

"Yes," Krashchenko agreed. He raised his wrist and displayed his watch to the group. "That means that Falconi and the Black Eagles have only seventy-two hours of life left to them."

2nd Lt. Betty Lou Pemberton and her nursing assistant Mrs. Jean McCorckel tenderly ministered to the badly wounded soldier on the bed in the Long Binh hospital ward.

Jean smiled at the young man. "Soon you be home."

The man grimaced as the two nurses went through the routine of preparing him for transportation. "Yeah," he said through clenched teeth. "And it can't happen too soon."

Betty Lou knew that the bandaging was causing him acute discomfort despite the fact she was doing the job with all the gentleness possible. The best thing was to get his mind off the ordeal. "Who'll meet you there, Greg?" she asked using his first name.

"Uh," he groaned. "I think my mom and dad for sure. Maybe my fiance – oh – if she can make it."

Jean held the end of the dressing while Betty Lou gently tied it as tightly as possible. "I never asked you where you were from? Or did I forget you told me."

"Philadelphia," the soldier said. "Ooh! That feels better now."

"That good," Jean said.

"Thanks a lot," the wounded man said sincerely. "It hurts like hell to put 'em on tight, but they always feel better afterward."

"You're welcome, Greg," Betty Lou said. "They'll be picking you up in another hour or so. We had to bundle you up for that trip. Can't have you unraveling on us, can we?"

He forced a grin. "I guess not. I suppose you've heard this before, but I gotta tell you. The two of you have been great."

"Part of the job," Betty Lou said. "And you can say it all you want. We love to hear it from you wonderful guys." She offered her hand. "It was nice knowing you. All the best, Greg."

Jean also shook hands with the man. "Maybe I see you when I go to United States."

"Oh, yeah!" the soldier said. "I forgot you were married to a GI, Mrs. McCorckel. You and your husband can drop in any time."

"You bet," Jean said. She gathered up the instruments and remnants of bandage rolls. "Goodbye."

"So long."

The two nurses walked up to the front of the ward. When they arrived at the small glassed-in office they found their reliefs had reported in.

"Glad to see you," Betty Lou said to the two newcomers. "It's been a long day."

"You want to get something to eat?" Jean asked.

Betty Lou sighed. "We might as well. We sure won't be dining with those men of ours for awhile."

"Don't worry," Jean said displaying a good humored grin of support. "We still have each other."

The two friends walked out of the hospital building and turned down the street toward the nearby PX snack bar. Although the establishment was staffed by native Vietnamese, the service was strictly American with a menu that consisted mostly of hamburgers, fries and milkshakes. This was where Jean had developed her rather novel ideas on the eating habits of United States citizens.

It only took ten minutes for them to go through the line and load their trays with a variety of junk food. The GIs in the place feasted their eyes on the two attractive women as they made their way through the tables to one in the far corner.

The nurses sat down, and Betty Lou took a sip of her thick chocolate milkshake. "If I keep eating like this I'm going to be as big as a cow."

Jean giggled. "Me too. But when Malcomb is

100

gone with Colonel Falconi I don't care."

"Me neither," Betty Lou said. "Although I wish I could have seen Archie before he left."

"Oh, too bad," Jean said. "But Malcomb say you speak to him on telephone, no?"

"Yes," Betty Lou said. "At least they let us do that." She took a bite of her cheeseburger and thoughtfully chewed for several moments. "Jean, is Malpractice—I mean Malcomb—going to stay in the army?"

"I think so," Jean answered. "He have a lot of years, Betty Lou."

"So has Archie," Betty Lou said. She was quiet for another short period. "Has Malcomb ever spoken of going back to the States?"

"Yes, sometimes," Jean said. "He thinks we will go to Fort Bragg. That's where the Special Forces are."

"What about leaving the Black Eagles?"

Jean nodded. "Yes. When we first met, Malcomb was very upset all the time. That was at my home in Tam Nuroc. Many, many Black Eagle die. He was afraid he lose more friends. So he talked to me about going to another unit and maybe work in hospital. You know, like the medical corpsmen on the ward."

Betty Lou closed her eyes. "That would be wonderful, Jean! No more worries. You could be stationed at a nice post like Fort Lewis or Fort Riley, living a very wonderful humdrum existence. It would be a nice life with weekends free. You could visit his family during furloughs, or go on trips, and live a normal life."

Jean shrugged. "But Malcomb go back to Black Eagles, Betty Lou. I think he stay until this war over."

"Over?" Betty Lou snapped. "This thing is going to go on forever!"

Jean, who had been witness to the fighting in Indo-China since her childhood, only smiled. "Maybe you right, Betty Lou." She took a drink of her tea. "What about Archie?"

Betty Lou's face was a mask of grief. "Archie will always be with Colonel Falconi," she said.

Jean reached out and laid her small hand on her friend's arm. "Something is wrong, Betty Lou?"

"Yes," she answered. "I feel that Archie is doomed. I really mean it, Jean. I don't think I'll ever see him again."

Jean, who believed strongly in premonitions and messages from the spirit world, gasped. "Do not think of it, dear Betty Lou!"

"Think of it—*think* of it?" Betty Lou asked. "Oh, Jean, I *know* it!"

Jean smiled sadly and reached out to lay her hand on Betty Lou's. "We must be soldiers like our men, Betty Lou," she said. "We also have to be brave—as brave as they are."

"Even braver," Betty Lou countered. "Our job is harder—we're the ones who have to wait."

Chapter 8

The rising sun was reflected as little red sparkles off the slick blanket of dew that covered the concrete apron in front of the hangar.

The Black Eagles' parachutes and field gear were neatly lined up in two rows like mute, stumpy little soldiers. The ominous M16 rifles, taped for the scheduled jump, were laid across the equipment. Gunnar the Gunner's M60 machine gun, securely put away in the large GP container, was also rigged for the airborne operation.

All of the weaponry and paraphernalia of war had been treated to a minute inspection by a combination team of CIA and KGB agents. These communist officers, all Russian, had been brought on board the base in a closed van. In spite of this precaution, they were still blindfolded and closely watched by alert MP guards. If the Reds found the experience unpleasant, they could console themselves with the thought that the CIA people were going through the same thing at the Red Bears' home station, since a similarly organized group would be doing the same thing to Krashchenko's detachment up north.

A mutual, vocal stamp of approval was given the stuff, then the intelligence people disappeared. Now the Black Eagles stood off to one side. With their bellies full of the hot breakfast brought out to them from a nearby USAF mess hall, they smoked and talked in low murmurs to each other. Their sergeant major, on the other hand, was deeply involved in his duties.

Top Gordon was performing a very special task that morning. The detachment's senior non-commissioned officer was doing the job as jumpmaster. This position, which was one that was regarded no less than sacred in the United States Army airborne, held a mystique that was perpetuated in paratrooper song and legend.

The jumpmaster's duties were clearly defined. Besides being required to be a graduate of an official jumpmaster qualification course, he is in command and has responsibility for all the parachutists in the aircraft in which he performs his duties. He must also assure that the airplane from which he and his fellow jumpers are about to exit, is safely and correctly prepared for the dangerous undertaking.

It was the duty of this high office that now occupied Sergeant Major Gordon's attention.

The first order of business was the inspection of the aircraft. In this case, it was a C-130. Top began with a simple walkaround, paying particular attention to the two exit doors. He made sure there were no protruding objects around the area. Top saw that the edges were securely taped and padded so that no sudden slapping of static line there would cause the opening device to break.

Top went inside and made his rounds there. He noted the floor was clean and that there was no liquid—such as spilled coffee by the air force crew, leaking hydraulic fluid, etc.—for the parachutists to slip on. He also made sure the seats were properly installed and each had a seat belt.

The air force crew chief, a technical sergeant, stepped down from the pilots cockpit. "Howdy."

Top turned and looked at him. "How're you doing?" He went to the lights and checked to see they were working properly. The red one was for warning the parachutists that the time to perform the jump was drawing near. The green one meant but one thing—Go!

The air force man was a veteran and knew the procedure. "We'll be dumping you guys at one thousand feet, right?" He went to the intercom and plugged in the headset, then tossed it over.

"That's the ticket," Top said. He spoke into the microphone. "Commo test."

"I read you five by," came a voice back from the "front office."

Top tossed the device back. "We'll be going CARP," he said referring to the method to be used to let the jumpers know when to perform their exit. In this case it would be the Calculated

Air Release Point. "How's your navigator?"

"Damned good man, Sergeant Major," the other NCO replied. "I've flown plenty of training missions with him out of Pope."

"Good," Top said. He gave the interior another look-see. "Seems to be in good shape."

"It *is* in good shape," the technical sergeant said. "This is my aircraft."

Top nodded. "That's good enough for me." He went back to the door and stepped down the ladder to the concrete. "Hey!" he yelled at the Black Eagles. "What the hell are you standing around for? You know when station time is scheduled. Goddamnit! Chute up!"

The detachment went into action. Acting in two-man buddy teams, they helped each other slip into their parachutes. Since there were seventeen of them, Top was the odd-man out. He got into his gear on his own, but had to get Malpractice McCorckel to cinch up his belly-band and put the quick-release fold in it.

"Okay," Top said once he was fitted out. "Let's form up in stick order. He waited as two lines were formed in front of him. Then he began a methodical inspection of each man, following the same procedure sixteen times.

The first was Lieutenant Colonel Falconi. Although he was the commanding officer, he had to subordinate himself to the jumpmaster before and during the flight. Once they were on the ground, Top would revert back to his regular duties as team leader of Top's Terrors.

The first thing Top checked was the helmet.

"Let's see if you got that pot fastened down right, sir." Next he dropped down to the canopy release assemblies, then traced the chest straps down into the quick-release assembly to make sure there were no twists.

"How'd I do, Top?" Falconi asked.

"I ain't finished yet, sir," Top growled as he checked the assembly to see that it was in the locked position with the safety fork inserted. "That's okay. And your waistband is correct."

"You see, Sergeant Major," Falconi joked. "I can do some things right."

Top grinned and went on to inspect the reserve parachute worn on the front of the rig. "Well, you got the ripcord on the right side. Remember that when your main malfunctions."

"Okay," Falconi said. "And if it doesn't work, you can have these brand new jump boots I'm wearing."

"If I have to pull 'em outta your bloody ass, I don't want 'em," Top joked. He finished the frontal position noting that the leg straps were properly strung up through the leg strap loops. "Turn around."

The inspection of the rear included the back-pack itself, and particularly the static line. This was the device which the deployment bag—which held the parachute canopy and suspension lines—was attached. If that didn't work, then everything else was a waste of time.

Top finished up. "You're looking good, Colonel. Have a nice one."

"Thanks, Top."

Ray Swift Elk had been talking to Paulo Garcia during Falconi's jumpmaster inspection, and hadn't noticed the Top had finished.

"Lieutenant!" Top snapped.

Swift Elk snapped his head around, then turned and walked up to the sergeant major. "Sorry about that."

"You're slow and sloppy, sir," Top said. "Now let's start with that helmet."

The Sioux Indian went through the inspection, then stepped aside for the next man. When Archie Dobbs, waddling under the weight of his gear, stepped up, Top looked at him. "How're you doing, Archie?"

"Fine, thanks, Top," Archie replied cheerfully.

"That's good to hear," Top said. "By the way, are you planning on getting married someday?"

Puzzled by the question, Archie nodded his head. "Uh – sure. I guess so."

"What about kids? If you get married, do you want to have kids?" Top asked.

"Naturally," Archie said.

Top smiled pleasantly. "From the way you have your leg straps crossed under your crotch, you'll never be a father, Archie." He suddenly yelled out. "Because they'll crush your balls, you fucking idiot! Now get outta here and crawl back into that parachute the right way!"

"Yes, Sergeant Major!" Archie exclaimed making a quick escape.

After that episode, Top continued the routine until he had checked out each and every man, straightening a twisted strap here, poking in a

108

pulled risor there, until he was satisfied they were properly chuted up. When the job was finally finished, even Archie was looking good.

"Reverse stick order," the sergeant major called out. "Board the aircraft."

It only took fifteen minutes for all seventeen parachutists to be buckled in and ready to go. The aircraft engines were kicked into life, then the C-130 taxied down to the take-off position at the proper runway.

The pilot revved up the props and the big airplane strained against its own brakes, seeming as if it were a living being eager to launch itself into the sky. The whole thing vibrated and roared as the Black Eagles instinctively leaned forward in anticipation for the take-off run.

Suddenly the C-130 lurched forward and began to rapidly roll, picking up speed. Less than three minutes later the friction with the ground disappeared, and the lumbering plane eased upward in a rapid gain of altitude.

Archie Dobbs, excited as hell about the prospect of adventure ahead of him, tilted his head back and sang out as loud as he could:

"Black Eagles, Black Eagles have you heard?"
I'm gonna jump from this big iron bird!"

Within moments all seventeen men were clapping their hands in unison as they sang out their chants as if on a PT run. But within ten minutes, the horse-play died off, and each man lapsed into his own private reverie as the C-130 took them closer and closer to whatever fate awaited them.

Falconi, Malpractice McCorckel and Archie Dobbs had one thing in common. They each daydreamed about the women they loved.

Falconi was now glad that Andrea had reappeared in his life. He'd have several affairs since her departure, but each of these romantic, lustful forays had only served to convince him of how deeply he really loved the beautiful Eurasian woman.

Jean dominated Malpractice's thoughts. He was a very sensitive man, hence his choice of becoming a medic, and his wife had proved a comfort to him. Jean provided a harbor in the stormy emotional seas he had experienced in the combat-ridden service he'd pulled with the Black Eagles.

Archie Dobbs' mind was filled with pictures of Betty Lou. He knew, deep in his heart, that their relationship was shaky. But he couldn't bring himself to make a final decision where their romance was headed. He feared he would soon be with his back to the proverbial wall, forced to choose between the Black Eagles and Betty Lou.

Across the aircraft, Ray Swift Elk did not entertain any peaceful or loving thoughts. He leaned back into the canvas harness of the seat with his eyes closed, and repeated Sioux war chants over and over in his mind as he went through the secret medicine routine he'd learned from his grandfather. Swift Elk might have been an "officer and a gentleman" through an act of congress, but he was an Indian warrior deep in his heart.

Paulo Garcia stared off in space and smoked as he wondered about the tuna fishing season back in San Diego. Gunnar Olson thought of his favorite Norwegian food — *lefsa* and *lutefisk* — and wished he was in his Minnesota home enjoying some that very moment. Blue Richards, on the other hand, hummed old fashioned hillbilly songs to himself to pass the time.

And then there was Tiny Burke, the huge ammo bearer who served Gunnar the Gunner's M60. His mind was completely and totally blank. Of all the Black Eagles on that airplane, Tiny was the most at peace with the world at that particular moment.

The air force technical sergeant appeared out of the "office" up front and walked down to Top Gordon's seat. He leaned over and shouted in the sergeant major's ear. "Twenty minutes out!"

Top nodded. He undid his seat belt and stood up. He and the tech sergeant grabbed the port door and pulled hard, sliding it up into the overhead. They repeated the procedure on the starboard side. The sudden increase in the engine noise caught everyone's attention — even Tiny's.

Top held up both hands and opened and closed them twice to give the signal — twenty minutes.

The time crawled by, as the men prepared themselves for the ordeal ahead.

Top held out both hands to show that there were ten minutes to go.

Now all seat belts were loosened, and the men

double-checked their helmets to make sure they were secure and in place. Again they waited while unintentionally staring daggers into Sergeant Major Gordon.

Then the jump was on.

Top took a deep breath and bellowed the first jump command. *"Get ready!"*

Everyone leaned forward, holding out the snap fasteners of their static lines.

"Stand up!"

They all got to their feet and turned to face the doors at the rear of the aircraft.

"Hook up!"

The snap fasteners were hooked to the anchor cable.

"Check your equipment! Check static lines!"

The Black Eagles complied, with the last jumpers in the eight-man sticks turning so the number seven men could inspect their backpacks.

"Sound off for equipment check!"

With the two sticks counting off simultaneously, Top monitored them to make sure everyone had sounded off with their number to indicate they were okay.

Now Top had a few seconds to wait. He grinned encouragement at the men and gave them the "thumbs up" signal. At the same time he kept an eye on the lights. The red one suddenly came on.

"Stand in the door!"

Falconi in the right door and Swift Elk in the left, swung into the openings. Tensed and waiting, both men looked out over the jungle that passed beneath them a thousand feet below.

Then the green light was lit.

"*Go!*" Top yelled out the most famous of all the jump commands. He watched the two sticks rush the door as the Black Eagles emptied the aircraft. He gave Blue Richards, the last man in the right stick particular attention.

When Blue hit the blast, Top was right behind him.

"Hut-thousand! Two-thousand! Three-thousand! Four-"

The T-10 parachute canopy came out of the deployment bag and filled with air, braking Top's fall. The sergeant major quickly checked the chute, then looked around him. Slightly below, and strung out in a tight column, the other sixteen parachutists slowly lowered toward the ground.

The Black Eagles were at war.

Chapter 9

Falconi watched as the detachment formed up to move off the drop zone. All the parachutes and jump gear, including the helmets, had been gathered up and buried. These fresh diggings were carefully camouflaged to avoid detection by any visitors to the scene. Sergeant Major Gordon supervised this "sterilization" of the DZ with his usual style and efficiency. This generally included yelling at Archie Dobbs every few minutes.

When that chore was finished, Falconi gave the word to move out. The machine gun team, Gunnar Olson, Tiny Burke and Sparks Johnson, stuck close to him as part of the command element. Archie Dobbs as the scout was glad for the opportunity to get away from Top Gordon. He had already moved to the head of the group to act as scout and pathfinder.

Ray's Roughnecks were the lead team with Top's Terrors in the middle. Calvin's Crapshooters handled the rear with the last man, Dean Fotopoulous, charged with the important responsibility of having to make sure no one hit them from behind. He would do a lot of looking over his shoulder as well as turning to walk backward now and then.

Falconi, from his center position, glanced up and down the column of his command. And he damned well liked what he saw. The Black Eagles were primed and ready for a dangerous undertaking, and had volunteered for with more than one hundred percent in numbers — they were there with a hundred and ten percent dedication and determination.

The colonel was proud at that moment, and he loved every one of the dirty brawling, drinking bastards with all his soldier's heart.

And the Black Eagle commander was most assuredly a soldier.

Robert Mikhailovich Falconi was born an Army brat at Fort Meade, Maryland in the year 1934.

His father, 2nd Lt. Michael Falconi was the son of Italian immigrants. The parents, Salvatore and Luciana Falconi, had wasted no time in instilling appreciation of America and the opportunities offered by the nation into the youngest son. They had already instilled deep patriotism into their seven other children. Mister Falconi even went as far as naming his son Michael rather than the Italian Michele. The boy had been born an American, was going to live as an American so — *per Dio e tutti i santi* — he was going to be named as an American!

Young Michael was certainly no disappointment to his parents or older brothers and sisters. He studied hard in school and excelled. He worked in the family's small shoe repair shop in New York City's Little Italy during the evenings, doing his homework late at night. When he graduated from high school, Michael was eligible for several scholarships to continue his education in college, but even with this help, it would have entailed great sacrifice on the part of his parents. Two older brothers, beginning promising careers as lawyers, could have helped out a bit, but Michael didn't want to be any more of a burden on his family than was absolutely necessary.

He knew of an alternative. The nation's service academies, West Point and Annapolis, offered free education to qualified young men. Michael, through the local ward boss, received a congressional appointment to take the examinations to attend the United States Military Academy.

He was successful in this endeavor and was appointed to the Corps of Cadets. West Point didn't give a damn about his humble origins. It didn't matter to the Academy whether his parents were poor immigrants or not. West Point also considered Cadet Michael Falconi as socially acceptable as anyone in the Corps regardless of the fact that his father was a struggling cobbler. The only thing that concerned the institution was whether he, as an individual, could cut it or

116

not. It was this measuring of a man by no other standards than his own abilities and talents that caused the young plebe to develop a sincere, lifelong love for the United States Army. He finished his career at the school in the upper third of his class, sporting the three chevrons and rockers of a brigade adjutant upon graduation.

Second Lieutenant Falconi was assigned to the Third Infantry Regiment at Fort Meade, Maryland. This unit was a ceremonial outfit that provided details for military funerals at Arlington National Cemetery, the guard for the Tomb of the Unknown Soldier and other official functions in the Washington, D.C. area.

The young shavetail enjoyed the bachelor's life in the nation's capital, and his duties as protocol officer, though not too demanding, were interesting. He was required to be present during social occasions that were official ceremonies of state. He coordinated the affairs and saw to it that all the political bigwigs and other brass attending them had a good time. He was doing exactly those duties at such a function when he met a young Russian Jewish refugee named Miriam Ananova Silberman.

She was a pretty, twenty-year old brunette, who had the most striking eyes that Michael Falconi had ever seen. He would always say throughout his life that it was her eyes that captured his heart. When he met her, Miriam was a member of the League of Jewish Refugees, attending a congressional dinner. She and her father, Rabbi Josef Silberman, had recently fled the Red dictator Stalin's anti-Semitic terrorism in the Soviet Union. Her organization had been lobbying the American Congress to enact legislation that would permit the US government to take action in saving European and Asian Jewry not only from the savagery of the communists but also from the Nazis in Germany who had only just begun their own program of intimidation and harassment of their country's Jewish population.

When the lieutenant met the refugee beauty at the start of the evening's activities, he fell hopelessly in love. He spent that entire evening as close to her as he could possibly be while ignoring his other duties. A couple of congressmen who arrived late had to scurry around looking for their tables without aid. Lieutenant Falconi's full attention was on Miriam. He was absolutely determined he would get better acquainted with this beautiful Russian. He begged her to dance with him at every opportunity, was solicitous about seeing to her refreshments and engaged her in conversation, doing his best to be witty and interesting.

He was successful.

Miriam Silberman was fascinated by this tall, dark, and most handsome young officer. She was so swept off her feet that she failed to play the usual coquettish little games employed by most women. His infectious smile and happy charm completely captivated the young belle.

The next day Michael began a serious courtship, determined to win her heart and marry the girl.

Josef Silberman, her father, was a cantankerous, elderly widower. He opposed the match from the beginning. As a Talmud scholar he wanted his only daughter to marry a nice Jewish boy. But Miriam took pains to point out to him that this was America—a country that existed in direct opposition to homogeneous customs. The mixing of nationalities and religions was not that unusual in this part of the world. The rabbi argued, stormed, forbade and demanded—but all for naught. In the end, so he would not lose the affection of his daughter, he gave his blessing. The couple was married in a non-religious ceremony at the Fort Meade post chapel.

A year later their only child, a son, was born. He was named Robert Mikhailovich.

The boy spent his youth on various army posts. There were only two times he lived in a town or civilian neighborhood. The first was during the years his father, by then a colonel, served overseas in the European Theater of Operations in the First Infantry Division—the Big Red One. A family joke developed out of the colonel's service in that particular outfit. Robert would ask his dad, "Why are you serving in the First Division?"

The colonel always answered, "Because I figured if I was going to be One, I might as well be a Big Red One."

It was one of those private family jokes that don't go over too well outside the home.

The second stint of civilian living was in San Diego, California during the time that the colonel was assigned as the supervisor of that city's public school Reserve Officer Training Program.

But despite this overabundance of martial neighborhoods, the boy had a happy childhood. The only problem was his dislike of school. Too many genes of ancient Hebrew warriors and Roman legionnaires danced through the youth's fiery soul. Robert was a kid who liked action, adventure and plenty of it. The only serious studying he ever did was in the karate classes he took when the family was stationed in Japan. He was accepted in one of that island nation's most prestigious martial arts academies where he excelled while evolving in a serious and skillful *karateka.*

His use of this fighting technique caused one of the ironies in his life. In the early 1950s, during the time his father headed up San Diego, California's high school ROTC program, Robert was himself a student – a most indifferent scholar at best. Always looking for excitement, his natural boldness got him into a run-in with some young Mexican-Americans. One of the Chicanos had never seen such devastation as that which Bobby Falconi dealt out with his hands. But the Latin-American kid hung in there, took his lumps and finally went down when several skillfully administered and lightning quick *shuto* chops slapped consciousness from his enraged mind.

A dozen years later, this same young gang

member named Manuel Rivera, once again met Robert Falconi. Rivera was a Special Forces sergeant first class and Falconi a captain in the same elite outfit. SFC Manuel Rivera, a Black Eagle, was killed in action during the raid on the prison camp in North Vietnam in 1964. His name is now listed on the Black Eagles Roll of Honor.

When Falconi graduated from high school in 1952, he immediately enlisted in the army. Although his father had wanted him to opt for West Point, the young man couldn't stand the thought of being stuck in any more classrooms. In fact, he didn't even want to be an officer. During his early days on army posts he had developed several friendships among career noncommissioned officers. He liked the attitude of these rough-and-tumble professional soldiers who drank, brawled and fornicated with wild abandon during their off-duty time. The sergeants' devil-may-care attitude seemed much more attractive to young Robert than the heavy responsibilities that seemed to make commissioned officers and their lives so serious and, at times, tedious.

After basic and advanced infantry training, he was shipped straight into the middle of the Korean War where he was assigned to the tough Second Infantry Division.

Falconi participated in two campaigns there. These were designated by the United States Army as: *Third Korean Winter* and *Korean Summer-Fall 1953*. Robert Falconi fought, roasted and froze in those turbulent months. His combat experience ranged from holding a hill during massive attacks by crazed Chinese Communist Forces, to the deadly cat-and-mouse activities of night patrols in enemy territory.

He returned stateside with a sergeancy, the Combat Infantryman's Badge, the Purple Heart, the Silver Star and the undeniable knowledge that he had been born and bred for just one life — that of a soldier.

His martial ambitions also had expanded. He now desired a commission but didn't want to sink himself into the curriculum of the United States Military Academy. His attitude toward schoolbooks remained the same — to hell with 'em!

At the end of his hitch in 1955, he re-enlisted and applied for Infantry Officers' Candidate School at Fort Benning, Georgia.

Falconi's time in OCS registered another success in his life. He excelled in all phases of the rigorous course. He recognized the need for work in the classrooms and soaked up the lessons through long hours of study while burning the midnight oil of infantry academia in quarters. The field exercises were a piece of cake for this combat veteran, but he was surprised to find out that, even with his war experience, the instructors had plenty to teach him.

His only setback occurred during "Fuck Your Buddy Week." That was a phase of the curriculum in which the candidates learned responsibility. Each man's conduct — or misconduct — was passed on to an individual designated as his buddy. If a candidate screwed up he wasn't punished. His buddy was. Thus, for the first time in many of these young men's lives, their personal conduct could bring joy or sorrow to others. Falconi's "buddy" was late to reveille one morning and he drew the demerit.

But this was the only black mark in an otherwise spotless six months spent at OCS. He came out number one in his class and was offered a regular Army commission. The brand-new second lieutenant happily accepted the honor and set out to begin this new phase of his career in an army he had learned to love as much as his father did.

His graduation didn't result in an immediate assignment to an active duty unit. Falconi found himself once more in school, but these were not filled with hours of poring over books. He attended jump school and earned the silver parachutists badge; next was ranger school where he won the coveted orange-and-black tab; then he was shipped down to Panama for jungle warfare school where he garnered yet one more insignia and qualification.

Following that he suffered another disappointment. Again, his desire to sink himself into a regular unit was thwarted. Because he held a regular army commission rather than a reserve one like his other classmates, Falconi was returned to Fort Benning to attend the Infantry School. The courses he took were designed to give him some thorough instruction in staff procedures. He came out on top here as well, but there was another thing that happened to him. His intellectual side finally blossomed.

The theory of military science, rather than complete practical application, began to fascinate him. During his time in combat—and the later Army schooling—he had begun to develop certain theories. With the exposure to Infantry School, he decided to do something about these ideas of his. He wrote several articles for the *Infantry Journal* about these thoughts—particularly on his personal analysis of the proper conduct of jungle and mountain operations involving insurgency and counterinsurgency forces.

The army was more than a little impressed with this first lieutenant (he had been promoted) and sent him back to Panama to serve on a special committee that would develop and publish US Army policy on small-unit combat operations in tropical climates. He honed his skills and tactical expertise during this time.

From there he volunteered for Special Forces—the Green Berets—and was accepted. After completing the officers' course at Fort Bragg, North Carolina, Falconi was finally assigned to a real unit for the first time since his commission. This was the Fifth Special Forces Group in the growing conflict in South Vietnam.

He earned his captaincy while working closely with ARVN units. He even helped to organize village militias to protect hamlets against the Viet Cong and North Vietnamese. Gradually his duties expanded until he organized and led several dangerous missions that involved deep penetration into territory controlled by the communist guerrillas.

It was after a series of these operations that he was linked up with the CIA officer Clayton Andrews. Between their joint efforts the Black Eagles had been brought into existence, and it was here Lt. Col. Robert Falconi now carried on his war against the communists.

Now the Black Eagles moved deeper into the jungle, following Archie Dobbs' northerly path as they headed for the rendezvous with the Red Bears. The men were silent, tending to their areas of responsibility while keeping close tabs on their individual team leaders in case any quick orders were signaled down the line.

The situation reminded Falconi of the poet Alan Seeger, an American who served in the French Foreign Legion during World War I. Seeger had written a poem about having a rendezvous with death, a work of art which unfortunately came true for the young man. He was killed in action on June 29, 1915 in an attack on a war-ravaged French village called Belloy-en-Santerre.

Falconi suddenly recalled the great clarity the lines of that poem about an inevitable tryst with death:

I have a rendezvous with death
At some disputed barricade,

When Spring came back with rustling shade
And apple blossoms fill the air—

I have a rendezvous with death
When spring brings back blue days and
fair—

And I to my pledged word am true,
I shall not fail that rendezvous.

Falconi glanced up and down the silent, plodding column of the Black Eagles. And he wondered who among them also had such a rendezvous.

Chapter 10

Krashchenko oscillated gently under the canopy of the Soviet PD-47 parachute as it lowered him toward the grassy drop zone. He took a quick look around to check out the rest of the Red Bears. About half had already landed and were busy rolling up their chutes while the others, like their KGB commanding officer, were still on their way to the ground.

Krashchenko's mind was suddenly occupied with the task at hand. He bent his legs slightly and prepared for the shock of the landing. There was only a slight breeze in the heavy tropical atmosphere, so the KGB colonel's impact with the ground was minimal. He rolled with the momentum of the fall, then got to his feet and freed himself from the harness. The first thing he grabbed was his AK-47. He was damned well angry about the slow manner in which the drop zone defensive perimeter was being organized.

Krashchenko signaled to the Bulgarian

Dzhurov. "Get the Third Section over to the north side quickly!" he ordered.

"Yes, Comrade Lieutenant Colonel!" Captain Dzhurov replied. He hustled his men along in their chore of untangling themselves from their jump equipment.

The Fourth Section, under the command of the East German Senior Lieutenant Deintz, was already moving out to take up their positions.

"Karlov!" Krashchenko barked. "Hurry up that section of yours."

"*Da, Tovarisch Podpolkovnik!*" Karlov shouted as he waved at Krashchenko. He immediately turned to kick the nearest of his command in the ass. "Move! Move! *Bistrieh!*"

His outfit, the Second Section, reacted too quickly to his angry orders by hastening their pace until they covered their area of security around the drop zone.

Meanwhile, Krashchenko's own First Section that included the three-man machine gun crew had also positioned itself. The entire Red Bear Detachment melted into the jungle area immediately around the drop zone, all alert and ready for any enemy movements.

The KGB border guardsman Ali Khail who acted as their scout was impatient. He crawled over to Krashchenko. "I volunteer for a patrol to inspect our surroundings, Comrade Lieutenant Colonel."

Krashchenko nodded his approval. "Very well, Comrade Sergeant. We are only wasting time sitting here."

Ali Khail crawled forward into the brush with all the skill he had developed during his years of patrolling the wildest areas of the Soviet Union's borders. Once he was deep into the jungle, he began a slow, careful circuit, keeping his black eyes darting back and forth as his ears stayed tuned for the sound of any potential attackers.

It took the renegade Cossack an hour to complete the task. When he returned to his commander, the sweat was streaming off his shaven head and seeping from under his wide-brimmed cap to leak down his brutal face. He preened his large, waxed moustache. "We are alone here, *Tovarisch Podpolkovnik.*"

"Very well," Krashchenko said. He turned to the two machine gunners who had the muzzle of the RPD trained outward. "We are moving out, Comrades."

The crew, both of the Russian naval infantry, was as efficient with their weapons as Ali Khail was at scouting. Within seconds they were standing up and ready to move out. Their security rifleman, the Polish paratrooper named Spichalski, covered them as they followed Krashchenko and the Cossack scout off the perimeter and deeper into the monsoon forest.

Krashchenko spoke into his hand-held R100 field radio. "Section Commanders, form the order of march."

Khail nodded a temporary goodbye to his commander and moved off to take up his position at the front of the column. Russian Major Karlov's Second Section was at the head of the formation with Krashchenko's First Section following. Next came Dzhurov's Third Section with the Fourth under Deintz bringing up the rear.

They formed a double-column with the men staggered along the formation so as to provide the best side security. The Red Bears, anxious to clash with the hated Black Eagles, were alert and eager as they moved slowly in their penetration of the operational area.

Their superb physical conditioning came to their aid as they traveled steadily through the steamy weather and stubborn vegetation that clung and grasped at their clothing and exposed skin. Grimly determined and anxious for combat, they pressed on without a break for two solid hours.

Ali Khail was a master man-tracker. Besides looking for possible enemy trouble nearby, he concentrated on evidence of any foe who might have ventured through the territory where he now led his comrades. His eyes searched almost frantically for some tell-tale sign such as a footprint, or even a bent blade of grass in his quest for some sign of the men they sought. The man was a natural killer-hunter, and craved slaying the game he now tracked. The fact that he scouted for human beings added fuel to his inner spark for combat.

Ali Khail used his nose too. Part of the Red Bears' training had included a close study of American characteristics. They knew the *Amerikanski* had a fondness for shaving lotion. Several popular brands had been on hand for examination, and the Cossack had spent plenty of time sniffing the contents of the bottles to familiarize himself with the peculiar odors the capitalists preferred.

But the first man-smell he perceived was not the sweet, heavy scent of after-shave. Instead, it was the stench of human feces.

Ali Khail, excited, whispered into the radio. *"Prival!"*

The entire Red Bear column halted and went to the ground. As each man covered his particular field of fire, he gave no thought to the relief of being able to rest. They were all too excited about the reason for the halt. Without exception, the Red Bears hoped the Americans had been discovered.

Krashchenko, just as anxious as his men to find out what the hell was going on, transmitted back to his scout. "What has alarmed you, Comrade Sergeant?"

"There are people nearby, Comrade Lieutenant Colonel," Ali Khail replied. "A great number, I think. I must go forward."

"We will wait," Krashchenko said.

Ali Khail, on his belly, demonstrated the patience that had made him so damned good at his job. He traveled forward in this uncomfortable position by inches. A half hour later he heard human speech. He listened intently, then radioed back to Krashchenko. "There are native people twenty meters to my front," he reported.

"Military?" Krashchenko asked.

"I think not, Comrade Lieutenant Colonel," Ali

Khail said. "I hear woman and children."

"There are supposed to be no villages in the operational area," Krashchenko said. "That is why it was chosen for this battle. Investigate and report to me as soon as possible."

"*Da, Tovarisch Podpolkovnik,*" Ali Khail replied in the affirmative.

The human noise was now loud enough that the KGB man could move faster without worrying about the sounds he was making. He came across an area obviously used as an open latrine of sorts. There were scores of human droppings. Ali Khail noticed they were mostly fresh and knew the group had not been in that particular spot for very long—and were not planning on staying any period of time either. That would explain the carelessness about sanitation.

A suddenly movement in the bushes startled him, and he ducked down. He glanced through some palm fronds and caught sight of a young woman. Ali Khail grinned to himself. This was the ladies' "bathroom."

The woman pulled up her long skirt and squatted down. She squinted and grunted with effort several times, the strain evident in her expression.

Again Ali Khail smiled. "*Zapor*—constipation," the scout whispered to himself. He enjoyed the sight of the woman's buttocks as she worked at the task. Finally she emitted a loud sigh as the bowel movement began. Even the Cossack was repelled by the sight. He turned away with a frown. When he looked back she was cleaning herself with a couple of broad leaves she'd brought for the purpose.

After the woman left, the border guard went around the open filth, and finally reached a good observation point. He watched the activity and made special mental notes as he studied the group of people before him.

There were about a hundred of them with possibly twenty being men. The others were women and children of various ages. As he had surmised, this was not a permanent village. These people were merely camping. The bundles of belongings within in their group were obviously rigged for carrying, thus they were engaged in a journey of sorts.

Ali Khail backed off a bit and transmitted his findings back to Krashchenko. The Russian lieutenant colonel wasted no time. "Karlov, take your section forward and secure that group of people on the south side. Dzhurov followed up on the north, while Deintz goes to the east. I will cover the west with my section. *Pripadok!*"

Within a quarter of an hour the Red Bears had quickly and silently pulled off the envelopment. The Vietnamese peasants were first aware they had been surrounded when Ali Khail boldly stepped into view. He called out to them in a combination of the Vietnamese language he had learned and Russian:

"Chao ong, Tovarisch!"

There were gasps from the men and audible cries from the women. They instinctively backed away from the foreigner, but within moments more of his kind stepped out of the jungle and arranged themselves around the camp. There was some more frantic milling around, but finally their headman stepped forward. He rightly picked out Krashchenko as being the leader. He walked up to him and nodded with a smile in the polite Oriental manner.

"Chao ong," the peasant leader said.

"I do not speak your language!" Krashchenko barked. During all the time he had been stationed in North Vietnam he had made not one effort to pick up a word of the Vietnamese native tongue. He considered the people barbarians and felt it was beneath the dignity of a commissioned officer of the KGB to fraternize with them.

The peasant, correctly assuming he was not being understood, bowed and tried in another language. *"Parlez-vous francais?"*

"Deintz!" Krashchenko yelled out. "Get over here!"

The East German officer quickly complied. "Yes, Comrade Lieutenant Colonel?"

"You are a linguist. Help me with this man," Krashchenko ordered.

"He asked if you spoke French," Deintz said.

"You speak that sissified language, don't you? Then act as the interpreter."

"Yes, Comrade Lieutenant Colonel. What is it that you wish to say to him?"

"Ask him what he is doing here?" Krashchenko said. "This obviously isn't his village."

"Yes, Comrade Lieutenant Colonel." Deintz looked down at the Vietnamese. *"Pourquoi sont*

134

vous ici?"

The man answered in long sentences gesturing and rolling his eyes. When he was finished he waited patiently while Deintz translated.

"He says that he and his people are fleeing the war," the East German said. "Their village has been burned down several times by both the army and the guerrillas. They are looking for some place to resettle where there is no fighting."

Krashchenko laughed. "He certainly made a mistake when he came here, didn't he?" Suddenly he glared at the peasant. "Ask him where he learned to speak the decadent language of the French."

Deintz spoke again, then turned to Krashchenko. "He tells me that he worked as a waiter in Hanoi, but came back south after the French left."

"Why did he not stay there and live under the fruits of communism?" Krashchenko asked.

Deintz's face was a mask of proper severity. "He must be a reactionary of sorts, *Tovarisch Podpolkovnik*. The dog says he thought he would find a better life in his home village where he grew up."

"Mmf!" Krashchenko snorted. "I will discuss that with him later. Right now we must see what he has observed during his journey out to this place." He turned to the Red Bears. "Sit these people down and keep your weapons trained on them. We are about to conduct some interrogations."

The headman smiled uncertainly and spoke

urgent words to Deintz.

"What did the little wog say?" Krashchenko asked.

"He wants to know what is going to happen to him and his people," Deintz replied.

"Tell him to take a walk with us," Krashchenko said. "We have some questions to put to him."

Deintz spoke rapidly to the Vietnamese. The peasant displayed polite resignation. The unfortunate man had been questioned by soldiers before.

Chapter 11

The first order of business for the Black Eagles after the infiltration and move away from the drop zone, was to establish a highly defensible base camp. It would have been unwise and dangerous to simply move into a war zone and casually roam around the area waiting to see what situation might develop.

Falconi, who did a map reconnaissance on the evening prior to the parachute jump, had already chosen an elevated area. The closeness of the contour lines on the topographic chart indicated a fairly steep hill. The green color promised covering vegetation that would require some clearing for fields of fire, but would make concealment much easier. Also, its distance from the drop zone was a plus in determining its value. If the infiltration had been observed, the enemy would not have been forced to travel far to catch up with the detachment.

Archie Dobbs, in his job as scout, was tasked with working out the proper azimuth to be followed from the drop zone to this chosen site. As usual, Archie's sense of direction was flawless.

Within an hour and a half of the infiltration, he led the detachment directly to the spot.

Archie raised Falconi on the Prick-Six radio. "Falcon, we're here. Over."

Falconi radioed back for the scout to wait. He went forward along the column until he reached its head. "Is this it, Archie?"

Archie pointed where the terrain made a steep rise from the surrounding ground. "Check your map, sir. We're home."

Falconi grinned. "I have a lot of faith in you, my boy. If you say this is the place, that's good enough for me."

When the Black Eagles moved up the hill and claimed it as their base camp there was no time for relaxation. An immediate and effective defense had to be implemented without delay. Due to the heavy plant growth in the area, the first thing was the clearing of those vital fields of fire. Failure to do so would drastically cut down the range of defensive fusillades.

This was one job that Gunnar the Gunner Olson took extremely seriously for his machine gun. He and Tiny Burke first chose a good central spot in which they could cover any side of the perimeter. They dug their position keeping in mind that there was every possibility they might have to physically shift the gun's position rather than simply turn the barrel toward any targets. That meant the tripod could not be weighted down with earth or other cover.

Next they went forward and hacked away brush that impeded their ability to get good sight pictures. Tiny, his heavily muscled torso gleaming with sweat, swung his machete with the regular rhythm of a machine.

Falconi formed his defense into a triangular formation. Ray's Roughnecks took the north side, Top's Terrors defended the southeast angle, and Calvin Culpepper positioned his Crapshooters along the southwest line. Every man dug a fighting hole and constructed a small hootch to the rear for sleeping and the storage of personal equipment. The latter was no more than having a poncho stretched out into an open tent, then storing gear under it leaving a place for their air mattresses, mosquito netting and poncho liners.

The next order of business was camouflage. The jungle itself gave good concealment, but the men had to concentrate on not ruining this natural cover. They preserved this by the selective cutting of brush used to hide the combat positions and hootches. The needed flora was taken at scattered areas far away from the actual camp. Facilities for disposing of trash and other refuse were also carefully constructed and concealed.

This entire chore, which would have taken a basic training company an entire day to accomplish, was complete within two hours. The men settled in with the exception of Archie Dobbs and a representative from each of the teams. Ray's Roughnecks donated Dwayne Simpson, Top sent Salty O'Rourke and Doc Robichaux showed up from Calvin's Crapshooters.

Defense is much more than simply digging in

and fortifying a position. The enemy must also be kept off balance out in No Man's Land. There is only one way to accomplish that, and such a job calls for aggressively patrolling. That was something that Lieutenant Colonel Falconi believed in to a great extent. Several of his articles in the *Infantry Journal* had strongly recommended the concept. He had called these four men exactly for such a task. It would have been nice to maintain team integrity by sending an entire group out on the mission, but that would have meant a side of the perimeter left open until filled by others. Instead, Falconi took one man from each of the fire teams. That still left each sub-unit with three, and Gunnar's M60 could make up for any unexpected need of extra firepower.

Falconi gathered the patrol around him. Each man had a map of his own and they referred to them from time to time as their commander conducted the briefing.

"We don't know what the enemy situation is," Falconi said. "We can assume that the Red Bears made their infiltration into this area at about the same time we did, though not at the exact moment. They might have been a bit earlier or a bit later."

Dwayne Simpson raised his hand. "Do you have any idea where their drop zone was, sir?"

Falconi shrugged. "I'm afraid not. But it wouldn't matter. I'm positive they did as we did and moved away from it as quickly as possible."

"If they're smart they did," Archie said menacingly.

"Right," Falconi agreed. "Now let me organize you people. The leader, by right of military rank, will be Salty."

"Aye, aye, sir!" Salty acknowledged.

"Next is Dwayne, then Doc," Falconi said. He laughed and pointed to Archie. "We all know what his rank is, right?"

"Don't say it!" Archie said. "Buck-assed private, okay? I know it, guys, and so does my wallet."

"Don't feel left out, Archie," Falconi said. "You're still the scout and get to lead physically."

"Thank you, sir," Archie said smugly.

Falconi got back to business. "This is a reconnaissance patrol. You know what that means, right?"

"Yes, sir," Doc Robichaux said. "We sneak and peek and avoid fire fights and other contact with the enemy."

"Exactly," Falconi said. "Your mission is twofold. You're to check out the area to the north and bring back any information on the terrain you can get to augment this map. There's always a stream or other natural feature that's not shown. The other part of the patrol order is the most important and the most dangerous. I want you to find those goddamned Red Bears and get back here with the information. And don't forget to count the sons of bitches. Let's also concentrate on their base camp, right? That means layout and dispersement of personnel on the perimeter. Be damned sure you locate their machine guns."

"Gotcha, sir," Archie said. "But that's going to take more than just an afternoon."

"That's why this is an RON — Remain Over Night," Falconi said. "You'll take enough rations to get by for twenty-four hours. I also advise some light sleeping gear. That's because I don't expect you guys to go without any sleep at all. Hell, exhausted men can't find their own asses with their hands. You'll have to get some rest. But on the other hand don't take that old rule about needing eight hours of sleep to heart. It's going to be dangerous out there. Those sons of bitches will be looking for us too."

Salty lit a cigar. "What about indigenous personnel?"

"There's not supposed to be any native people in this area," Falconi said. "But if you see any, presume they are hostile."

"How much ammo should we take?" Dwayne asked.

"Don't overload yourselves," Falconi said. "One bandoleer will be plenty. I want you to strip down to the bare essentials. No more than a patrol harness. And remember — no personal effects outside of your dogtags. Leave your wallets behind."

"There ain't nothing in them anyhow, sir," Archie reminded him. "Top had us strip 'em out back at Peterson Field."

"Don't take them anyway," Falconi said. "Any carelessness could account for a scrap of paper or some other intelligence left inside. It's safer this

142

way." He checked his watch. "I want you moving out within fifteen minutes."

Salty looked at his own timepiece. "I guess you'll expect us back at this time tomorrow."

Falconi nodded. "When I say twenty-four hours, I mean it. I want to see your ugly mugs coming in through this perimeter at *exactly* this time tomorrow."

"Aye, aye, sir," Salty said.

"Make it a good one, guys," Falconi said. "Move out!"

Podpolkovnik Gregori Krashchenko's patience was stretched to the limit. He pushed past Deintz who had been ineffectively interrogating the headman of the village for the previous half hour.

"You stinking bumpkin!" he screamed in rage. "I'll show you what happens when you attempt to dally with the KGB!"

The Vietnamese bowed several times toward the raging Russian. "*Xin loi ong!* I am sorry! But I know nothing to tell to you gentlemen." He turned a pleading face toward the East German. "*S'il vous plait, monsieur* — please!"

Deintz sneered at the man, but he shrugged. "He says he knows nothing, Comrade Lieutenant Colonel. I am inclined to believe him."

"Nonsense!" Krashchenko snapped. "Are you letting him fool you, Deintz?"

The German paled, and he replied in Russian. "*Nyet, Tovarisch Podpolkovnik!* But I have been using all my skills as an interrogator."

Krashchenko laughed disdainfully. "Your Nazi SS would certainly not be impressed by such puny efforts. How do you think the men of the German death's head regiments might handle this situation?"

Deintz was indignant. "They were not my SS, Comrade Lieutenant Colonel."

"You are German!" Krashchenko yelled. "And they were German! I won't argue with you about this. Now answer me! How do you think an SS officer would react to this slant-eyed little bastard?"

Deintz gritted his teeth and held his temper. "The SS fascists would undoubtedly take hostages."

"Excellent," Krashchenko said. "We will follow your countrymen's historical example." He yelled out to his scout and rifleman. "Ali Khail! Spichalski! Go grab three of the wogs and bring them here."

The duo, who had been standing nearby in listless boredom, quickly leaped to life. They rushed past the line of guards and charged into the group of sitting natives. The Red Bears selected three men. They grabbed them by the arms, and hauled them to their feet. The women immediately began screaming and crying. A couple reached out to grab their men, but were savagely kicked away. The three hapless prisoners were pushed and pummeled out of the crowd and back where Lieutenant Colonel Krashchenko waited for them.

The village headman saw what was happening. His judgment of the situation was not based on historical references toward the SS. The Vietnamese man knew the communist method from first hand experience. He looked at Krashchenko, a man with whom he could not communicate. The only hope—as slim as it was—laid with the German. At least he could talk to him. *"Monsieur,* please tell your commander that I know nothing about any soldiers in this area. I have seen none. I ask you and I beg you, *monsieur,* show mercy to my people. They are innocent. If you must punish someone, do it to me."

Krashchenko's irritation grew. "What did he say?"

Deintz, who was beginning to believe he might be getting on the KGB man's bad side, didn't care to elaborate. "He is only repeating himself, *Tovarisch Podpolkovnik!"*

Krashchenko ordered the hostages' hands to be bound behind their backs. He glanced back to Deintz. "Tell him to answer our question or we shall shoot one of them."

Deintz translated the threat into French. The Vietnamese trembled and he began to weep. "It is not their fault. Shoot me instead!"

Deintz spat. "He will not speak, Comrade Lieutenant Colonel."

"Ali Khail!" Krashchenko barked. "Shoot the first man."

"Da Tovarisch Podpolkovnik!" the Cossack replied. Without hesitation he raised his AK47 and pulled the trigger. The weapon was on full auto-

matic, and a quarter of the magazine's contents slammed into the back of the prisoner. Bloody meat and shattered ribs exploded outward from his body before he fell heavily to the ground.

The headman acted decisively then. That terrible atrocity showed there was no hope for him or his people. It was time for a desperate move. He suddenly broke loose and ran toward his people. *"Nguy-hiem!"* he shrieked. "Run for your lives!"

There was a sudden surge of humanity as the people leaped to their feet and fled toward the jungle. This unexpected action caused a moment of confusion among the Red Bears guarding the natives.

Ali Khail, on the other hand, didn't waste a beat as he turned his weapon on the other two hostages. Their attempt at escape lasted less than three paces before they were blown down by a single volley of skillfully aimed fire.

"You bastard!" Krashchenko bellowed at the headman. The KGB officer ran after the native and easily caught up with him. He drew his Tokarev pistol and aimed it straight at the man's head.

The Vietnamese sneered openly now. "You cowardly dog!"

Krashchenko looked at Deintz. "What did he say?"

"He is begging for mercy," Deintz wisely lied.

Krashchenko laughed and pulled the trigger. The bullet slapped into the headman's skull, blowing bits of bloody brains onto the brush behind him.

Meanwhile, the other Red Bears began to act. The first orders were issued by the Bulgarian Dzhurov. "Fire! Fire! Fire!" he screamed hysterically.

His own Third Section were the first to obey. Their fusillades cut into the backs of the villagers as they left the clearing and disappeared into the jungle. The unlucky ones were knocked down by the swarm of bullets, but the more fortunate among them gained the safety of the trees.

By then Krashchenko had rushed across the open space to join the Bulgarian.

"Dzhurov!" he yelled. "Take your men after them." He motioned to the other section leader. "Karlov, you follow. I'll come along after you with my machine gun team and Deintz' men."

Archie Dobbs heard the shooting and signaled a halt. Salty O'Rourke moved forward and joined him. "What the hell do you think it is?" the marine staff sergeant asked.

"I don't know," Archie said. "But Falconi said we was a recon patrol, right?"

Salty grinned and winked. "Right! So let's go recon." He turned and signaled the others to follow as Archie stepped off toward the sound of increased firing.

Chapter 12

Jean McCorckel finally learned to cook other American dishes besides hamburgers and french fries.

Luckily for her, she had a good teacher. Archie Dobbs' girlfriend Betty Lou Pemberton was an excellent cook. The army nurse introduced Jean to the mysteries of a great Stateside repast — roast beef, mashed potatoes and gravy.

This culinary lesson took place in Andrea Thuy's kitchen. The Eurasian woman had formed a deep friendship with both Jean and Betty Lou. After all, the three attractive women all had one thing in common: their lovers were in the Black Eagle Detachment.

Andrea's apartment in the *Quartier des Colons* section of Saigon was small, but air conditioned. In spite of this touch of modernization and comfort, the heat coming out of the little stove still made the small cooking area too uncomfortable to remain there very long. The women gamely stuck to their posts, however, and worked at the meal while wiping the perspiration from their foreheads, and consuming large glasses of iced water.

Betty Lou opened the oven door. The delicious odors of the cooking meat wafted out. Jean, standing directly behind her, leaned forward and sniffed. "Ah, Betty Lou! It smells delicious!"

Andrea Thuy stood in the door of the kitchen. She agreed. "I haven't smelled anything that good since my last trip to the States."

"This is real American home-style cooking," Betty Lou said spooning up some of the gravy from the bottom of the pan and pouring it over the roast. "Any mother back home will tell you that it's food like this that gets our girls their husbands."

Andrea laughed. "And I always thought it was trapping the poor guys with feminine guile."

"And big breasts!" Jean added with a giggle.

Betty Lou closed the oven. "Now, girls. Let's not get dirty," she said joining in the joke. "Whew! The meat is coming along fine, so let's get out of here and cool off while we have the chance."

"Good idea," Andrea agreed leading her two friends out into the apartment's main room. The drop in temperature was quite noticeable in this area that served as a combination living and dining room. At that particular moment, a large table dominated the room. Normally it was kept off to one side of the room with its leaves folded down, but Andrea had set it up for this very special meal.

There were four place settings arranged on the clean, white cloth that covered it. As if noting the extra one for the guest who had yet to arrive, Andrea commented, "I wonder when Fagin is going to get here."

"Yeah," Betty Lou said thinking of Archie. "I hope he has some news for us."

"*Good* news!" Andrea emphasized, with her own thoughts on Robert Falconi.

"Of course," Jean said. Her husband SFC Malpractice McCorckel was the object of her concern, but she gave little evidence of feeling uneasy about his situation. This was not the first time she had been worried about a war situation. Having been raised in the town of Tam Nuroc on the Song Cai River, she'd been close enough to battle to have to dodge the bullets herself. The young Vietnamese woman knew that needless fretting was the worst thing a person could do. Sensing that the light mood might quickly darken, she quickly changed the subject. "Now let me see if I remember," she said pointing to the silverware. "There is a salad fork, regular fork, spoon, knife and soup spoon. Correct?"

"Yes, Jean," Betty Lou said. She pointed to another eating utensil. "You forgot this one."

"Easy," Jean said with a laugh. "That is the butter knife, no?"

"It is the butter knife, yes!"

Andrea decided to keep the now elevated atmosphere in full swing. "Okay, you charming ladies, it's drinky-poo time. Name your poison."

"Oh, Andrea!" Jean exclaimed. "I do not want to take any kind of poison!"

Betty Lou laughed and slipped an arm around her Vietnamese friend's waist. "It's a joke, Jean. That's the way Americans ask what kind of alcoholic drink you want."

"You people are so strange," Jean said with a giggle. "But I will take one scotch with some soda."

"Make that two," Betty Lou said.

"I'll make it three," Andrea said going over to the liquor cabinet. She took out a bottle of scotch, then also grabbed a fifth of Irish whiskey. "I might as well leave this out. I bought it for Chuck Fagin. When he wants to drink, that guy does it hard and fast without amenities." She quickly made the requested drinks using ice from an ice bucket sitting on the table. The container, a souvenir from some old friends in a French para regiment, was decorated with their parachutist wings on one side and the famous beret badge of a winged hand holding a dagger on the other.

Betty Lou pointed at it. "You'd better get one of those with the Black Eagle insignia, Andrea."

"Believe me" Andrea replied. "When they make one I'll be the first to get it."

"Unsung heroes," Betty Lou said. "I'm afraid that describes our boys to the proverbial 'T.' "

"Too bad," Andrea said. "The American public will never know about them."

"Perhaps after the war there'll be an opportunity for the people in the USA to learn about them," Betty Lou mused thoughtfully.

Within moments, all three women had been served their drinks. Betty Lou raised her glass. "Here's to the one thing we need the most of — luck!"

"*Chuc co may man!*" Jean said repeating the toast in Vietnamese.

"*Bonne chance!*" Andrea added in French.

"What about Spanish?" Betty Lou asked. "I learned that in high school. *Buenas suerte!*"

"As the Norwegians say, *til lykee!*" Andrea exclaimed.

"Where in the world did you learn that?" Betty Lou asked.

"From Gunnar Olson," Andrea answered.

"You really have a talent for language," Betty Lou exclaimed. "I had so much trouble with—"

She was interrupted by a knock on the door.

Andrea pulled a .45 automatic pistol hidden behind the bottles in the liquor cabinet. "You two move back against the wall. This may appear to be; melodramatic, but trust me when I say it's necessary."

Her two friends quickly and silently did as she asked.

Andrea went to the peephole and peered out in the hall. "God! He's so ugly!"

"I heard that!" came Fagin's voice from the hallway. "Let me in, you insulting wench."

Andrea opened the door and admitted the CIA case officer. He stopped in the doorway and leered at them. "Wow! Three good-looking women!" Then he sniffed the air. "Is that roast beef? I think I died and went to heaven."

Andrea returned the weapon to its hiding place. "You get nothing to eat until you bring us up to date on the Black Eagles."

"Okay," Fagin said. "I'll do my best, but you know their mission, as always, is highly classified."

"For God's sake!" exclaimed Betty Lou. "Then tell us what you can!"

"I can't say much except that they're now committed and are on the ground in the operational area."

"Did the parachute jump go okay?" Betty Lou asked.

"Yeah," Fagin said. "All the guys are up and running around."

Jean took a nervous sip of her drink. "Has there been fighting, Chuck Fagin?"

He shook his head. "None to report, Jean." He looked at her. "How come you always call me by both my names?"

Jean shrugged. "I don't know, Chuck Fagin. Does it offend you?"

"Hell, no, Jean McCorckel," he said. "So I'm going to call you by both yours."

"Sure," she said. "I like everybody to know that I am Malcomb's wife."

"I definitely don't understand *that!*" Fagin said. He turned to Andrea. "Feed me!"

She pointed to the Irish whiskey waiting for him. "What about that?"

He walked over to the bottle and pulled the stopper out. He put the fifth of liquor to his mouth and took four deep swallows. Then he set it down and wiped his mouth. "Now, for the love of God, feed me!"

Archie Dobbs' senses were screaming at him in silent cries of warning. The hair on the back of his neck stood up, and goose bumps ran up and down his spine.

He slowed down the patrol to such an extent that Salty O'Rourke angrily moved forward to find out what was going on. He knelt down beside the scout. "What the hell are you waiting for? The goddamned Welcome Wagon?"

"We're getting close to something," Archie lamely explained.

"Close to what, goddamnit?" Salty asked. He glanced around him. "I don't see nothing and I don't hear nothing, Archie. So how about stepping up the pace, huh?"

Archie scowled back at him. "I don't see or hear nothing either, Salty. But I sure as hell *feel* something."

Salty started to argue with him, then calmed down. "Okay, Archie. I been out in the field with you once before, and I learned to listen to you. Go on and do what you think best."

Archie nodded and turned to resume the slow pace as he led the recon patrol deeper into unknown and unfriendly territory. For the next quarter of an hour the jungle seemed normal. Birds flew and insects whirred about. Then suddenly the most ominous warning of something occurred.

Silence!

Archie immediately signaled a halt. Salty and Dwayne went to the earth and each covered a flank. Doc, in the rear, dropped down and turned in that direction.

Only a couple of seconds later there was evidence of a great disturbance approaching them. The crush of vegetation could be heard, then shrill yelling and crying.

Salty looked up toward Archie. "Sounds like women and kids."

"Yeah," Archie agreed puzzled.

The first of the peasants burst into view in the clearing directly in front of Archie. It was a young woman carrying a child. Her eyes were wild and wide with fright. Immediately behind her came some more children, then a group of women. Running wildly and obviously in great fear, they sped across the space.

Archie stepped out. *"Durng lai!"* he called out in their language.

The people in front came to a halt while those behind piled into them. Several were knocked to the ground and they scrambled desperately back to their feet. Three of them turned to run back from where they'd come, but realized that was no good. They, like the others, now milled in confusion in the cleared area.

"What are you running from?" Archie asked.

Salty, Dwayne and Doc joined him. Salty took no chances and put the two out to the front as lookouts.

One of the women, braver than the others, trembled with anxiety, but she answered loudly. "Soldiers!"

"What soldiers?" Archie asked.

His question was answered when Dwayne and Doc fired into the jungle and came back into the clearing.

"There's two bandits coming this way!" Doc said.

Then a duo of uniformed men suddenly burst into view. Salty's patrol could not fire at them for fear of hitting the non-combatants between the two groups.

The Red Bears were as surprised as the Black Eagles. But, unlike the quartet of Americans, they felt no hesitation in shooting.

Archie and the others leaped back into the protection of the jungle on their side of the clearing. Bullets slapped into the vegetation around them. A couple of screams showed that stray rounds had slammed into the pitiful crowd of women and children. This caused another panic among the civilians and they began their wild, mindless rush for safety once again.

Archie tried to fire, but his aim was ruined by the people who rushed past his gunsights. Now two more of the enemy troopers in their camouflaged uniforms appeared to add to the volume of incoming volleys.

A young woman, leading an older child by the hand, was hit in the side. She staggered sideways as the girl with her held on in desperation. A couple of more slugs slammed into her and both fell to the ground. The youngster raised her head in time to have it split apart in another fusillade. Both mother and daughter died together.

Now, with the non-combatants gone, the Black Eagles returned the cowardly, wanton shooting. The ferocity of the sudden full-automatic return fire caught the communist soldiers by surprise. Their commander, Captain Dzhurov, gave immediate orders to fall back into the cover offered by the thick monsoon forest.

Archie, hearing the shouted instructions, turned his muzzle toward the senior man and hosed a long fire burst at him. "No more women and kids here, asshole!" he bellowed at him.

A furious exchange of shots followed, then gradually died off. Salty chanced a look from his firing position. "I think they've withdrawn."

"Right," Archie agreed. "How about some recon by fire, Salty?"

"Good idea," Salty said. "Colonel Falconi said this was a reconnaissance patrol, didn't he? So cut loose!"

Four M16s were emptied in the enemy area, then fresh magazines were slapped into the weapons. The procedure was repeated twice more before the Black Eagles were satisfied the Reds had withdrawn.

"Cease fire!" Salty said. "They're gone. It was a good tactical decision on their part. The bastards didn't know if there were more of us coming up or not."

Doc Robichaux reached in his pocket for his chewing tobacco. "Say, Salty," he said biting off a chaw. "We didn't know if there was more of them either. How come we didn't pull back?"

"Because I'm a goddamned marine and I don't believe in moving backward," Salty said.

Archie took advantage of the breather to treat himself to a drink of water from his canteen. "Did you guys get a good look at them sonofabitches? They had a red bear insignia sewed over their jacket pocket. Them's our boys all right."

"You bet," Dwayne Simpson said. "Archie, can you pinpoint our location on the map?"

"Yeah," Archie said. "I'd say this here recon patrol has accomplished its mission. We found 'em."

"Right," Salty said. "Let's head back, boys. This information is gonna put our little war into high gear." He looked around. "I wonder where them women and kids are running to."

Archie laughed. "Salty, they'll be at our base camp before we will." He shifted his rifle and stepped out. "C'mon, boys, let's go see the boss man."

Chapter 13

Top Gordon shifted the stogie in his mouth as he moved slowly forward, his M16 rifle locked and loaded with the muzzle pointed outward for immediate action.

The sergeant major was pulling a one-man perimeter patrol in front of his position. Back on the Black Eagles' main line, Malpractice McCorckel and Blue Richards stayed on the alert while their team leader made his rounds. Malpractice had his Prick-Six radio turned on, barely able to hear the hissing of empty air coming through the earpiece.

Top, walking softly, moved with the easy grace of an experienced jungle fighter. He had made a circuit around the entire base camp, being careful to check in with each fire team before he walked in front of their positions. Soldiers, even veterans like the Black Eagles, could be trigger-happy in a "shoot first, ask questions later" situation like they were in. And Top sure as hell didn't want to take a chance of getting blown away by his own men.

This seemed like a simple matter that would be no cause for nervousness. But the fact was, the NCO didn't have the slightest idea of who — or how many — nasty people might be out there.

Top made no sound as he began his second go-round. Then he stopped.

What was that he just heard? Running feet coming like hell through the brush? He frowned in irritation. If Archie Dobbs suddenly appeared leading that recon patrol back in such an amateurish fashion, he'd have the scout's ass for sure.

But Top heard something else — a child's cry!

He quickly pulled up his own radio. "Falcon, this is Falcon Two, over."

Falconi's voice came on the air. "Yeah, Falcon Two?"

"We got civilians — sounds like a lot of women and kids — approaching the position. Over," Top reported.

The radio's distortion of Falconi's speech did not hide the irritation in it. "Falcon Two, what the hell are you talking about? There're not supposed to be any civilians in this area. Over."

"Falcon, I swear to God that I hear kids squawking and crying. I say again — no shit. Over."

"Stay where you are," Falconi said. "I'll send two guys to help you hem 'em in between you and the perimeter. Out."

Top squatted down and nervously waited for

whatever was going to happen. A couple of minutes had gone by when Gunnar the Gunner Olson and Tiny Burke showed up. Gunnar, as usual, acted as the spokesman. "The old man sent us out to help you."

"Yeah," Top said. "There's a bunch of non-combatants heading this way. We're gonna—"

But before he could finish the sentence, a large crowd of loud Vietnamese drew alarmingly close. They suddenly burst into view in front of the three Black Eagles.

Top jumped up and beckoned Gunnar and Tiny to follow. "Scare 'em toward the camp!"

All three bellowed and ran toward the civilians. More shrieking followed, and the crowd was herded through the trees until they stumbled across the perimeter and into the camp.

Malpractice McCorckel, his medical corpsman instincts rushing to the surface, jumped out of his hole. "Hey!" he yelled out at nobody in particular. "Some o' them kids are wounded! A coupla women too!"

Hank Valverde and Dean Fotopoulus came in from Calvin Culpepper's side of the line. Now the civilians were surrounded and cut off from further escape. The frightened women and children crowded together in a frantic mob.

Falconi saw that a real case of mass hysteria was about to break. "Hey!" he yelled out at the top of his voice. *"Durng lai!"* he yelled out in Vietnamese. "Sit down and be quiet! *Mau len!"* He hated like hell to be so stern and forceful, but he had no choice. The situation could quickly get out of hand.

The sudden explosive sound of the booming male voice caught their attention. The people quickly squatted down. The only sounds were some soft, uncontrollable sobbing by a few of the women, and some crying kids.

"Who is in charge here?" Falconi asked, continuing to use the Vietnamese language. "I wish to speak to the senior lady present."

There was a hurried consultation among the women. Finally an older lady stood up. She slowly shuffled forward, her head bent in a submissive gesture. When she reached Falconi, the woman bowed repeatedly. "*Chao ong*," she said.

Falconi nodded his head. "*Chao ba*," he replied politely. "I am *Trung-Ta* Falconi."

"I am *Ba* Ling."

"How do you do, Mrs. Ling. Will you tell me, please, what you are doing here?"

"We run from the war, *Trung-Ta*," Mrs. Ling explained.

"You are running from where?" Falconi asked.

"Far away to the *dong*—the east—is our home village," Mrs. Ling explained. "The soldiers from the government visited us many times. They collected taxes and took young men to fight with them in the war. Then the guerrillas came. They also collected taxes and took away the youths. We decided to run away where no soldiers could find us." She began to weep in utter misery. "But we have failed!" Mrs. Ling finally regained some control. She looked up into Falconi's face. "We ask from you and your soldiers a favor, *Trung-*

162

Ta," she said. "The young women will not resist you. We ask only for consideration of their modesty. Please enjoy them out of sight of the children. You will have the pleasure you seek, and our girls will not fight back. I promise they will be submissive and cooperate with what your soldiers want."

Falconi shook his head. "Mrs. Ling, we are not going to outrage the women. We will help you." He pointed over to the edge of the crowd. "See? Even now our *bac-si* is looking after your children." He referred to the medic Malpractice as a doctor. Although it was a small white lie, it would give the unfortunate people a degree of comfort to think that a fully qualified MD was seeing after their health needs. It would also help the Black Eagle medic pursue his duties in cases where a woman patient might be required to disrobe.

Mrs. Ling turned to see Malpractice tenderly ministering to an injured youngster. He spoke poor, but passable Vietnamese. The expression on the face of the child's mother gave every indication she was very grateful.

"Our *bac-si* will tend to all your injuries," Falconi said. Now, since the preliminary and most necessary business was taken care of, it was time to slow down and let things proceed at the normal pace for Vietnam. "Would you like some tea, Mrs. Lee?"

"*Cam on ong*," the lady said.

"And will you have something to eat?" Falconi asked. "We have enough for everyone."

"Cam on ong," Mrs. Lee said expressing her gratitude.

Within twenty minutes, all the people were hungrily devouring a good portion of the Black Eagles' C-rations. There would be no resupply during the remainder of the operation, but not one man in the detachment complained.

Finally, after the correct amount of time had passed, Falconi got back to business. "Where are your men, Mrs. Ling? Surely they did not send you out in this wilderness by yourselves."

"They are with the other soldiers," she answered with great frankness. "But they are not as nice as you." She started crying again. "I think they killed all our men."

"What other soldiers? Were they white men?"

Mrs. Ling nodded. "Yes. But I do not believe they spoke the same language. There was much babbling and translating among themselves."

Falconi, in his eagerness, leaned forward. "Did they wear uniforms like ours?"

"Only similar," Mrs. Ling reported. "And they had a sign sewn on the chest."

"What sort of sign?" Falconi asked.

"It was red and was a fat tiger without a tail."

Falconi grinned — a red bear. "Mrs. Ling," he counseled her. "There is going to be a big battle."

The Vietnamese lady gasped.

"But," Falconi said to reassure her, "you and the other ladies and the children will be kept in safe places. We will take care of you and give you food and medical treatment. And, when we are able, you will be taken to a place to live where

164

there is no danger from battles. There are many villages newly set up for people like you."

"*Cam on ong!*" Mrs. Ling exclaimed.

"But you must obey us," Falconi said. "But every order we give will be for your own good. *Ba hieu khong?*"

"Yes, I understand," Mrs. Ling said.

"Fine," Falconi said standing up. He helped the lady to her feet. "Now let's go see how your injured people are doing."

The two walked over to Malpractice who was now bandaging a woman's badly injured arm. The medic, as usual, was lost in his work. Malpractice McCorckel, at times like that, didn't give a damn about politics, war or other human conflicts. All he cared about was giving comfort and aid while saving as many lives as he possibly could.

Gunnar the Gunner shifted the bore of the M60 machine gun. Tiny Burke beside him instinctively lifted the belt of ammo that had been fed into the automatic weapon's receiver.

"*Calcitras!*" Gunnar whispered out.

"*Clunis!*" came back Archie Dobb's correct reply to the challenge.

"C'mon across," Gunnar invited.

Archie moved through the gloom and reached the machine gunner's position. "Hi ya, Gunnar. There's three more guys coming in."

"Right, Archie."

That final bit of information was deadly important. It informed the perimeter guards of the number of men that made up the patrol. If any interlopers attempted to join the formation and infiltrate the area, they would be quickly caught.

Salty O'Rourke came across the defenses and gave Gunnar a wink.

"*En*," Gunnar said doing his count in Norwegian.

Next Dwayne Simpson entered the Black Eagle camp. "Hey, Gunnar. What's happenin'?"

"*To.*"

Dwayne looked back at the machine gunner. "Say, what?"

Tiny Burke grinned. "He's counting in Scandahoovian. It keeps him from getting homesick."

"*Tre*," Gunnar said noting Doc Robichaux.

Doc grinned. "Hey, I ain't *tre*, baby. I'm a Cajun, so that makes me *trois*." He turned around and faced outward. "Now let's make sure there ain't *quatre*, huh?"

"You mean *fire*," Gunnar said.

Dwayne spat. "You dumbasses. You both mean 'four', so why the hell don't you say so?"

Salty O'Rourke came back to the perimeter and scowled at Doc and Dwayne. "What the hell are you two hanging around here for? We got a patrol report to make. Do you think Falconi likes sitting on his ass waiting for you. He's a lieutenant colonel, so move your tails, goddamnit!"

The patrol members hurried after the marine. Falconi was waiting for them at his hootch, smoking a cigarette between sips of hot chocolate.

Archie, enjoying his own final smoke before it got too dark to strike a match, pointed outward as the rest of the patrol joined them. "Look. There's them women and kids those Red Bears was chasing."

Salty gave his report in a typical marine corps style. Gruff, concise, complete and without any extra, unnecessary detail.

Falconi was silent for a few moments while his mind digested the intelligence. When he spoke, he let everyone know he had already made a decision. "I'm going to send the Roughnecks and the Terrors out to make combat contact."

"Sounds like a job for Super Scout," Archie said. "I know where to take 'em, sir."

But Falconi shook his head. "You're too tired right now, Archie. I want you to enjoy a breather and try to get some snooze time."

"Aw, hell, Colonel!" Archie protested. "I ain't a bit bushed."

Falconi grinned at the scout. He knew that Archie rarely slept or ate on ops anyway. "Okay, eager beaver. You can go. In the meantime, fetch Ray and Top over here *pronto.*"

"Damnit," Dwayne Simpson swore. "There goes some more foreign language talking." Then he realized he was speaking to his commanding officer. "But I like it, sir! I consider it real educational."

Doc explained, "Dwayne got up tight about me and Gunnar counting in Norwegian and French."

"Well, shit!" Dwayne said defending himself. "There ain't nothin' wrong with 'one', 'two', 'three', is there?"

Before anyone could answer, Archie came back with Ray Swift Elk and Top Gordon. Ray squatted down beside Falconi. "What's happening, sir?"

"We've located Krashchenko's bunch," Falconi said not mincing words. "I'm sending your team and Top's out to kick some ass."

"You'll know 'em when you see 'em," Archie said. "But they ain't wearing red carnations in their lapels. The sonofbitches got red bears sewed on their jackets."

Top was pragmatic at such times. "You're going to send two teams instead of the whole detachment?"

Falconi pointed to the Vietnamese women and children. "I've got to hold back some people to protect the base camp for our guests. When things get hairy, pull a retrograde movement directly back here."

"When?" Swift Elk asked. "You sound like you're damned sure the situation is going to be a bad one."

"Right," Falconi said. "And those bastards will be right behind you. When they hit this camp we'll give 'em the surprise of their lives."

"Risky," Top flatly stated. "Damned risky."

"Are you **questioning** the mission, Sergeant Major?" Falconi asked.

"I only got one question, sir—when do we leave?" Top said.

"First light in the morning," Falconi answered. "Archie will be your point man. He's already made some personal acquaintances among the Red Bears."

Swift Elk glanced over at the scout. "Are they charming fellows, Archie?"

"Sure!" Archie said enthusiastically. "Let's go out there and kill 'em!"

"The sooner we start, the sooner it will be over," Swift Elk said.

"Yeah!" Dwayne Simpson chimed in. "One way or the other, brother. This campaign is gonna produce two kinds o' folks. Those that's livin' and those that's dead.

Chapter 14

Archie Dobbs was the first Black Eagle to actually see a Red Bear close enough to note his features.

Since the Black Eagles' intrepid scout spent most of his time at the forefront of the unit's activities, this was not too surprising. Archie caught sight of Ali Khail's brutal face, complete with waxed handlebar moustache, at the same instant the KGB border guard sergeant saw him.

Their brief, explosive exchange of shots started the first big battle of the secret campaign.

Lieutenant Swift Elk, as the senior ranking man, was the appointed leader of the Black Eagle combat patrol. He had already laid out preliminary plans with Top Gordon, who was the second in command, and the tactical conception immediately went into effect with the Sioux Indian's shouted command:

"Execute! Execute!"

Paulo Garcia, the Roughnecks' automatic rifleman, and Jessie Makalue, on the right side of the American line, made an encircling pivot around the enemy using Grenadier Dwayne Simpson as an anchor. Because of the arrangement of no rifle grenades, however, his role had been changed to that of automatic rifleman. Dwayne coordinated with them, covering their movement with his M16 selector switch on full-auto, primed and ready for any necessary action.

Over on the left, Salty O'Rourke performed those same automatic rifleman chores while Malpractice McCorckel and Blue Richards executed the necessary pincer maneuvers that were designed to act like human pliers.

The Red Bears, as was expected, were in a column formation. The head of their unit, Russian Maj. Pavel Karlov's Second Section, caught hell in the ensuing crossfire from the enveloping Black Eagles. Completely unready for the unexpected attack, they were caught flat-footed.

But Karlov was a well-trained infantry leader. *"Otdeplivat*—pull back!" he ordered.

His magnificently trained unit responded quickly, throwing out a covering fire from their AK47s as they withdrew in a tight formation.

Paulo swept the area ahead of him with well-aimed fire, gauging his shots as he allowed a good amount of lead for the running targets. He caught brief glimpses of the Red Bears' camouflage uniforms through the thick foliage, but was not rewarded with seeing his bullets hit any of them.

Now, with Lt. Col. Gregori Krashchenko in the

picture, the Red Bears formed up for the battle. Going quickly into line, their machine gun crew situated itself a bit back in their position. Then the RPD gun hosed out support fire for the men to the front.

Archie Dobbs, Swift Elk, Dwayne, Top and Salty charged forward but were forced back by the ferocity of the return fire. Salty, in his rage, cut loose with long fire bursts of eight and ten rounds. But the incoming machine fire was keeping him pinned down too close to the earth, so he was unable to aim properly. The slugs sailed harmlessly off into the bushes.

On the other side of the battle, Krashchenko kept in constant communication with his section leaders. He took their sporadic, uncoordinated reports and brought everything together in his mind. When he considered the time right, he uttered terse orders into the R100 radio:

"Pripadok — attack!"

The communist force leaped forward as one man and pressed through the trees. On their left flank, the attacking Americans, caught in the ferocious counter-assault, succeeded in pulling back, but on their right the Red Bears managed to cut off one Black Eagle.

Jessie Makalue knew he'd been separated when he lost visual contact with Paulo. In jungle warfare, distances are measured in meters not kilometers or miles. The big Hawaiian stayed cool and emptied the few remaining bullets in his magazine at the Red Bears who now turned toward him. Preparing to make a run for it, he shoved in a fresh magazine of thirty rounds, hit the charging handle and fired again.

The butt of the M16 pushed reassuringly against his shoulder with each round he shot at the fleeting figures in front of him. Then suddenly, he was punched in the stomach. Jessie grimaced and fired some more, then he received another haymaker. This time in the leg.

Growing confused, he looked down and noted the heavy flow of blood that was soaking his midsection. He dully noted that his pistol belt had been shot in two and was crazily swinging in front of him as it hung by the suspenders of his patrol harness. The Hawaiian's knees suddenly went weak and he staggered backward like a drunken man, falling down at the base of a large tree.

"Ain't this some shit?" he said to himself. He struggled valiantly and got back to his feet. Again he spotted the enemy advancing toward him through the jungle's heavy vegetation. He tried to raise his M16, but it was too heavy. His strength seemed to be ebbing away like the tide on an island beach. Gritting his teeth and sucking in air, he made another attempt, but even his hands were so weak that he couldn't hold onto the weapon. It slipped from his grasp and he fell back to a sitting position.

The Red Bear burst through the brush and stood in front of him. Dzhurov, the Bulgarian captain, started to fire but noted that the American had dropped his weapon. Here was a chance for a prisoner to interrogate. "Don't moof or I shoot you, meester," Dzhurov said in his broken English.

Jessie, his eyes wide open, looked blankly up into the Bulgarian's face.

Dzhurov moved forward very cautiously, ready for any trick. Then he stopped. One of the men from his section joined him. "Do you have a prisoner, Comrade Major?"

Dzhurov shrugged. He leaned forward and placed a hand on the side of the American's neck to feel for a pulse. "No prisoner here, comrade. This one is dead."

Fresh firing broke out to their left. They could barely hear the shouted commands of Krashchenko as he directed the attack against the Americans.

"Let us join the battle, comrade," Dzhurov said. "Get the others in the section."

"*Da, Tovarisch Mayor!*" the soldier responded.

Swift Elk hadn't been surprised by the Red onslaught. He pulled back both his fire teams and solidified his defenses. At that point in the fight, he wanted to test the Red Bears a bit. It was a fighting custom of his Sioux ancestors. Many times they gave pony soldiers opportunities to get aggressive in their actions to just to see not only what the white men would do, but how far they would go.

Krashchenko didn't know a damned thing about the plains Indians, he only knew that the enemy was to his front. He urged his section leaders forward as his three-man machine gun crew followed closely to give fire support.

Archie Dobbs was in the center of the line, as usual, and had taken cover in the roots of a gnarled ancient *rung* tree. Once more he caught sight of the mustachioed Red Bear he'd seen when the fight started. Archie got off a couple of quick shots and forced the man to take cover.

"How do you like them apples, Mustachio?" Archie yelled gleefully.

Ali Khail, the KGB scout, responded by rolling to one side and leaping up to deliver a quick volley of shots before diving to cover once again.

This time it was Archie who had to go low. "Russki motherfucker!" he bellowed. He took a grenade off the loop on his ammo pouch. Quickly pulling the pin, he held tightly onto the spoon, then let it loose.

"One, two, three, four—" Archie heaved the device as hard as he could and ducked even lower. A couple of beats later, there was an explosion. Archie quickly jumped up.

But the mustachioed commie was waiting for him. Grinning, Ali Khail sent an entire magazine of rounds zipping toward Archie.

Archie scrambled among the roots as the incoming bullets pinged and zapped around him for what seemed an eternity. When they finally stopped, he tilted his head back and shouted, "Think you're smart, don't you, asshole? Well, I know what you look like, and I'll be keeping an eye out for you."

Ali Khail didn't understand the words being shouted at him, but he had no doubt that their content was not complimentary. The Cossack sergeant yelled back a couple of Russian insults, then laughed crazily.

Now the rest of the line really exploded in a vicious exchange of fire. The Red Bears pressed their attack, but the return fusillades of the Black Eagles slowed them down, then caused them to halt altogether.

Swift Elk put in a call to Top. Two minutes later the sergeant major joined him in his position. Top had a bloody bandage around his head.

"Did you get hit?" Swift Elk asked.

"Naw," Top said. "Nothing that glorious. I ran into a tree limb. Malpractice slapped this on me."

"Glad you're okay," Swift Elk said. "We got to haul ass outta here. We're outnumbered right now, and Paulo told me that Jessie got cut off."

"Shit!" Top swore. "If he's out there he's either a prisoner or dead."

"We can't take him back one way or the other," Swift Elk said. "Our best chance is to launch an attack, then break it off and haul ass back for about a hundred meters. Then we can form up and pull off a proper retrograde movement."

"You're right," Top agreed. "It'll slow up the sons of bitches and make honest men out of 'em."

"Okay. We move out—" Swift Elk checked the hands on his watch. "—five minutes from— mark!"

"Gotcha," Top said noting his own timepiece. "No time to waste. See you a hundred meters back."

"Right, Top."

The word of the impending attack was passed

176

rapidly down the Black Eagle ranks despite the noise and activity going on in the exchange of fire with the Red Bears. Within four minutes all Black Eagles were poised to launch the assault.

Back on the communist side of the fight, Krashchenko personally directed the efforts of each of the line sections. His machine gun team kept up a steady rhythmic beat of 7.62 slugs out to the front. The KGB colonel bellowed over at the East German. "Deintz! Move your volleys to the right!"

"*Ja, Herr Kamarad Oberstleutnant!*" he replied in German. Then he quickly repeated himself in Russian. "*Da, Tovarisch Podpolkovnik!*"

Krashchenko crawled over to Dzhurov's section. "*Koroschi*—Good, Comrade Captain. You and your men are doing an excellent job."

The Bulgarian, like all his countrymen, loved to toady up to Russians. "Thank you, *Tovarisch Podpolkovnik*, and we can do even better!" He turned toward his men. "Increase your fire, you louts! Make every shot count!"

Krashchenko was about to holler some instructions to Karlov and the 2nd Section when all hell broke loose along the line.

The Black Eagles, after a brief but telling increase in their rate of fire, charged forward. Every man was on full automatic. The object of their fusillades did not count so much on accuracy as it did on the volume of bullets produced. They double-timed toward the Red Bear line, sending out swaths of 5.56 millimeter slugs that slapped through the air like scores of shrieking steel insects. Small limbs spun crazily off trees and the air was full of leaves and dust.

The Red Bears, despite their fanaticism, stopped shooting as the man-made hailstorm swept over them. The volume of noise and incoming fusillade of roaring hell forced them lower to the ground. Even Krashchenko hugged the dirt, his teeth tightly clenched. But he knew that his men were ineffective at that moment, and the situation could turn quite deadly for them. Now was the time for a good example.

"*Pripadok!*" he said, ordering them forward as he leaped to his feet. But even he was forced back down. The firing seemed to suck the oxygen from the air and turn the area into a vacuum.

Ray Swift Elk, a few steps behind the attacking Black Eagles, suddenly ordered the assault halted. It was the signal for each man to immediately stop the advance, then turn and run like hell for a hundred meters.

Archie Dobbs and Malpractice McCorckel had ended up together. The two old buddies bumped shoulders as they raced to the rear as fast as the jungle would permit. Both dully noted the complete absence of sound from the communist position, but didn't waste any breath on commenting on it.

After a hundred meters, Swift Elk turned. "Hold it. Get down and lay out some more fire."

The order was instantly obeyed. Another curtain of fire blasted outward from the Americans. After two minutes, Swift Elk ordered another withdrawal.

By the time the second hundred meters was reached, it was obvious that contact with the enemy had been broken. The Black Eagles formed up in column and began the rapid return back to the base camp.

"Well," Swift Elk said to Archie. "We handled them that time."

"Yeah," Archie said. "I recognized one of them fuckers, and I hope that mustachioed sonofabitch is still alive. I want to be the one who sends him to that great workers' paradise in the sky."

Paulo Garcia, walking beside them, grinned over at the scout. "Tsk! Tsk! Archie, are you taking things personally now?"

"Damned straight," Archie replied seriously.

"Don't worry about it," Swift Elk said. "You'll get your chance. Today was just the beginning, brother. Just the fucking beginning."

Chapter 15

The Red Bears, gathered around the dead man sprawled on the ground, were surprised at the physical size of the corpse. Ali Khail rolled the cadaver over and noted the muscularity that was obvious even in death.

"He is not of European ancestry," Ali Khail remarked in a matter-of-fact tone.

"Is he Vietnamese?" Karlov asked. "Or perhaps he is one of the Korean mercenaries hired to fight in this war for the imperialists." The Russian major looked carefully at the dead man. "He seems Oriental somehow, yet too large."

"The running dog was one of the Polynesian races," Krashchenko said. "No doubt he is a descendant of slaves who labored on the pineapple plantations in Hawaii for capitalist masters. I would believe he was duped by propaganda into serving the Wall Street gangsters."

Dzhurov and Deintz brought their two sections up and set up them up to join Karlov's men in an informal defensive perimeter. The section leaders saluted their commander. Dzhurov was in a good mood. "We scored a victory today, *Tovarisch Podpolkovnik*," he said.

Krashchenko didn't share his elated spirits. "We have evidence of only one death from the Black Eagle detachment. I would have hoped for more."

Deintz displayed his Teutonic pragmatism. "They are skillful fighters like us, Comrade Lieutenant Colonel. A great many shots were fired by both sides. They lost but one man and we none."

"We do not even have any wounded," Karlov reminded the other Russian. "This puts us ahead of Falconi and his capitalist gangsters."

"A small point has been scored," Krashchenko said, "but, as you all have said, it is a victory of sorts. Ali Khail followed their tracks for some distance until he was certain they had completely broken contact with us and withdrawn."

Dzhurov was satisfied. "We made them run then!"

"Perhaps," the Red Bear commander said. "But I have questioned several men from each section. I have come to the conclusion that the entire Black Eagle Detachment was not present at today's battle. For some reason, Falconi held back some of his troops."

"Ah, *da!*" Karlov agreed. "Did you notice there was no machine gun fire coming from their line? And they, like us, brought one with them into this campaign."

"Well observed," Krashchenko said in praise of his countryman. "I do not wish to be an alarmist, but this whole thing has made me suspicious."

Deintz shrugged. "But what sort of plan could Falconi be employing?"

"I intend to find out," Krashchenko said. "Perhaps he thinks we are stupid enough to believe we outnumber him by a great deal. On the other hand, this might have been part of a trap to lure us into an ambush where his machine gun would be waiting."

"Your last statement is the most logical, Comrade Lieutenant Colonel," Dzhurov said.

Krashchenko looked over toward his Cossack scout. "Ali Khail!"

The KGB border guard trotted over and saluted. *"Da, Tovarisch Podpolkovnik?"*

"We are going to trail the Black Eagles," Krashchenko said. "But discreetly and at a distance in case they have laid a trap. I want you to take the point position and proceed cautiously. Understand?"

"Akuratni, da! Do we leave now?"

"In a half hour. I want everyone to eat before we leave. I plan to travel without stopping for a great length of time. Also make sure they have ammunition and rations for three days. Do not forget to fill the canteens with fresh water. I want no unnecessary delays while we are on the move. Now see to your sections, quickly."

The three subordinate leaders saluted, then turned to prepare their units for the coming activities.

Andrea rapped on Chuck Fagin's office door

and stepped inside. Her face was pale and drawn. "Taggart has sent a runner to fetch us."

Fagin, a smoking cigarette between his nicotine-stained fingers, looked up from his paperwork. "Is it a report on Falconi and the guys?"

"The man didn't say, but what else could it be?" Andrea said. "Please hurry."

Fagin understood her anxiety. "C'mon then, Andrea." He got up and followed her out the door.

Despite having an escort, they still had to go through the prescribed security routine. It was ten full minutes before they walked into Brigadier General Taggart's office.

The general, behind his desk, gestured to his liquor cabinet. "Help yourselves."

"Sure," Fagin said heading for the scotch.

But Andrea was in no mood for alcoholic refreshments. "We're anxious to find out why you've sent for us," she said. "Is it about Falconi—that is, the Black Eagles?"

"Sure as hell is," Taggart said. "Looks like one of 'em may have bought the farm."

Fagin spun around so fast he spilled his drink. Both he and Andrea spoke simultaneously. "Which one?"

Taggart reached for the message in front of him. "A guy named—shit, how do you pronounce it? Ma— Maka—"

"Makalue," Fagin said.

"That's the one. Must be Hawaiian, huh?" Taggart said. "That's a damned shame. The army

183

gets good soldiers from the islands."

"Is he KIA?" Fagin asked.

"We don't know," Taggart said. "He's officially listed as missing." The general hesitated. "Maybe I should rephrase that since the Black Eagles have no legal recognition."

"Fuck that silly game," Fagin said.

"That's just part of the bad news anyhow," Taggart said.

Andrea's hands were tightly clasped together. "What else?" she asked. "Is someone wounded?"

"Nope," Taggart said. "That would be simple. It seems that our boy Falconi is loaded down with a bunch of Vietnamese women and children."

"Civilians?" Fagin exclaimed. "Impossible. All intelligence reports on the operational area assured us that the entire countryside was uninhabited. That's one reason it was chosen."

Taggart shook his head and displayed a sardonic smile. "These particular people were fleeing the fighting when they ran smack dab into the Red Bears."

"Oh, God!" Andrea said. She'd had plenty of horrible experiences with communist troops both as a child and an adult. "I presume the noncombatants are with Falconi because their men were killed."

"Absolutely right," Taggart said. "The problem is that the Black Eagles have an extra load with those people. It's like swimming with lead weights on your legs, know what I mean?"

"Shit!" Fagin swore. He took a deep gulp of the straight scotch in his glass. "If I know Falconi, he won't drive 'em off either. That crazy bastard will try to take care of them and win the god-damned war too."

Andrea's eyes blazed with pride. "Of course he will! Would you expect anything less from Robert?"

Taggart's eyes widened, and he turned his gaze on Andrea. "Are you and Falconi friendly, Captain Thuy?"

She took a deep breath. "Yes."

"How friendly?" Taggart asked tensely. "And don't give me any of that 'it's none of your business' shit."

"I'm a professional, General," Andrea said. "I realize the implications of Robert Falconi and I being lovers."

"Goddamnit! Are you lovers?"

"*Yes!* Goddamnit, yes!" Andrea shouted back.

Fagin stepped between them. "Ever'body kind of back off now, okay?" He looked at the general. "I've known they were an item for a long time, General. That's exactly why I pulled Andrea out of the cold and made her my administrative assistant. And she's been damned valuable in that job too."

"Hell, yes, I know that," Taggart agreed. "But somebody should have told me."

Fagin smiled. "Sorry about that. It just never came up in our conversations."

Taggart calmed down. "What the hell? As long as you're aware of the situation, I'm not going to worry about it."

"There's nothing to be concerned about," Fagin

assured him. "Now. What we have to consider here is Falconi's situation in the field."

"There's no problem," Taggart said. "We're going to order Falconi to drive those women and kids away."

"He won't do it," Andrea snapped.

"Then I'll court-martial his goddamned ass!" Taggart snarled.

"No you won't," Fagin said calmly. "In the first place his clandestine assignment precludes any court-martial. And even if he was nailed by the judge advocate general, how do you think the folks back home would like to hear about an American officer being punished for protecting innocent civilians in a war zone? Hell, the government is having enough trouble with war protesters now."

"Fagin, if Falconi doesn't get rid of them he'll get wiped out," Taggart reminded him. "It's be tough enough to fight that particular battle unhindered. Those Red Bears are some real bad asses."

"Falconi will do his best to take care of those women and children," Andrea said defiantly.

Taggart looked at her. "Then, my dear Captain Thuy, your lover is going to get his ass blown away!"

Andrea gritted her teeth. "I love Robert Falconi with all my heart. But I would rather have him die than survive over the bodies of women and children." She turned and faced Fagin. "Shall we go, Chuck?"

"Whatever you say, lady."

Ali Khail took the binoculars down from his eyes. He grinned evilly and slowly eased his way back through the brush. When he'd gone twenty meters, he stepped up his pace to report back to Krashchenko.

The Red Bears, occupying an impromptu but well concealed position, watched eagerly as the KGB border tracker hurried into the area.

Krashchenko, as impatient as his men, shifted his AK47 and turned to take the report. "Yes, Ali Khail. What have you found?"

The Cossack was pleased with himself. "I have discovered nothing less than the Black Eagles' base camp, *Tovarisch Podpolkovnik*. I am certain of that."

"Describe it to me," Krashchenko said.

"They are cleverly camouflaged, Comrade Lieutenant Colonel," Ali Khail. "But I spent an hour watching them. They have a defensive perimeter shaped like a triangle, thus—" He squatted down and cleared away a small area on the ground. He drew a diagram of the camp. "There appears to be a section on each side. Here, in the center, is that machine gun. It is situated so that the crew can swing it to cover any side of their defensive lines."

"What is your estimation of those defenses?" Krashchenko asked.

"Very strong, *Tovarisch Podpolkovnik*," Ali Khail said. "In fact, under normal circumstances, it would be suicidal for us to assault them there."

187

Krashchenko's curiosity perked up a bit. "What do you mean 'normal circumstances'?"

"You will not believe this, Comrade Lieutenant Colonel, but the same native women and children who fled from our socialist justice are now residing within that camp."

The news was so good that Krashchenko could not make himself believe it completely. "Are you sure?"

"I saw them with my own eyes," Ali Khail insisted.

Krashchenko dismissed it. "Never mind. If we attack, he will drive them away."

But the Cossack shook his head. "*Nyet*—no! They are clearly residing there, Comrade Lieutenant Colonel. Those whores and their brats have constructed small shelters. I even saw a man who appeared to be a *brach medik* treating some injured children. He had gone so far as to build a place to act as a rustic dispensary."

Krashchenko laughed softly. "Falconi was always a sentimental fool! There are times when a man must be hard as steel, and turn his heart to stone. That is something Falconi could never do, and that will be the cause of his ultimate destruction."

"*Tovarisch Podpolkovnik,*" Ali Khail said. "If we launch an immediate attack, the Black Eagles will be so encumbered with the women and children, it will be impossible for them to fight back effectively. Even their machine gun support will be curtailed. We could overrun them in less than a half hour."

"Exactly!" Krashchenko said happily. "Fetch the section leaders and bring them to me. We are going to move forward at once and storm the Black Eagle camp."

"This campaign is now over and we have won it," Ali Khail said.

Krashchenko nodded his agreement. "Comrade Sergeant, in forty-eight hours we, and this entire Red Bear Detachment, will be in Moscow drinking vodka toasts to our awards of 'Hero of the Soviet Union' medals."

"*Da!*" Ali Khail said. "On the other hand, the only honors for Falconi's Black Eagles will be the playing of taps over their graves."

Chapter 16

The women, crouching low in the shelters dug for them by the Black Eagles, tried to calm their terrified children. Scores of incoming rounds zipped overhead, slapping into the ground or zinging off as ricochets.

The noise was deafening, and any lulls in the roar of the shooting were filled in by shouted commands of Falconi or one of his team leaders.

Gunnar and Tiny, both grimly efficient, rock-and-rolled with the M60 to send out covering fire over the front line of defense manned by the three rifle teams. Both men worked hard from having to constantly shift their position to cover different areas as the fighting built up then died off along various points of the perimeter.

Archie Dobbs and Sparks Johnson, both extra rifles in the Command Element, also did their best to judge which side of the defensive needed extra firepower at any given moment. When they were a bit slow, there was no problem: Falconi made their decisions for them.

"Archie! Sparks! Get your asses over behind the Roughnecks!"

The two dutifully crawled in that direction and joined Ray Swift Elk's men in repelling a savage attack against their position.

"Archie! Sparks!" Falconi yelled again. "The Crapshooters need a hand."

Then the two supernumeraries, streaked with sweat and breathing hard, turned around and joined Calvin Culpepper's team for a bit of extra-curricular shooting.

No sooner had they begun working there, than Top's Terrors became hard pressed. Archie and Sparks, damning their own safety, rushed across the middle of the camp and dove in between Malpractice and Blue.

Outside, in the jungle Lieutenant Colonel Krashchenko directed these various forays. Although conducted by different sections, Ali Khail had participated in each attack. Krashchenko had assigned him the dangerous task of going up against each side of the Black Eagle perimeter to judge the strength and firepower on all lines of defense.

The Cossack, a bit winded from the effort, left the assaulting troops after the third attack. Despite his fatigue, he trotted at a rapid pace to report back to his boss. "I have now hit all sides of the Black Eagle defenses, *Tovarisch Podpolkovnik.*"

"Which side do you recommend we strike for the main thrust, *Tovarisch Serzhant?*"

191

Ali Khail did not hesitate. "The north side, Comrade Lieutenant Colonel. There seems to be one less man there. That may not seem like too great a difference, but in a small battle like this pressed into a compact space, a missing rifle could mean the difference between holding or caving in under the pressure of spirited storm troops."

Krashchenko was thoughtful. "Of course. No doubt that is the section where the dead Polynesian was assigned. *Koroschi* – good! Then that is where we shall launch our main attack. Call Dzhurov and Deintz to me."

Da, Tovarisch Podpolkovnik!" Ali Khail now forgot how tired he was in the excitement generated by a planned main thrust against the Black Eagles' weak side. He rushed off to fetch the officers.

Back on the other side, in the Black Eagle camp, Falconi was beginning to worry about the women and children. Although under cover, they were in a position to catch the brunt of the battle's roaring noise. It was a situation that could do more than simply frighten them – it could drive the unfortunate people mad with fear. The detachment commander got on his Prick-Six radio and called Top.

The sergeant major, enjoying the brief breather in the battle, quickly answered. "Yeah, Falcon. This is Eagle Two. Over."

"Eagle Two, can you spare the medic to look after those little guests of ours? Over."

"Affirmative, Falcon. But I may want to get

him back here in a hell of a hurry! Over."

"You call the shots," Falconi said into the mouthpiece. "But I want him to give them as close an inspection as possible, then report to me. Out."

Top crawled over to Malpractice's hole and nudged him. "Falconi wants you to give them women and kids a look-see. Then get over to the Command Element and tell Colonel Falconi what you find. And keep your ears open for the sound of my charming voice. If I want you back, I'll holler."

"Roger that, Top," Malpractice said. He slid out of his fighting position and raced to the middle of the perimeter where the Vietnamese were.

He found the oldest lady, Mrs. Ling, located in the center of the civilians. She was holding a baby in her arms. The child's mother, a young woman in her late teens, sat in listless shock beside them. Mrs. Ling smiled bravely up at the medic. "*Chao ong, Bac-Si.*"

"*Chao ba Ling,*" Malpractice said. "How is everybody doing?" Has anyone been hurt?"

"Not by bullets, *Bac-Si,*" Mrs. Ling answered. "But the noise is most frightening."

"Everyone must be brave and calm," Malpractice told her. "We will win this fight. Please, don't worry."

Mrs. Ling was not optimistic. "The battle has just started, *Bac-Si,* and I fear that some of the women may panic and try to run away."

Malpractice shook his head. "No, no, *Ba Ling!*" he said with great emphasis. "That would be

193

very *nguy-hiem* – dangerous! If they try to flee, the stray bullets will shoot them down as sure as if they were aimed at them."

"I have told them that," Mrs. Ling. "But they are so afraid." She pointed to the woman beside her. "See this one? Her husband was one of those killed by the bad soldiers. Now her mind is almost gone." Now the old lady wiped at her own tears. "We have been too much afraid for so long!"

"I understand," Malpractice said kindly. "We will protect you, but you must do as we say. *Ba hieu khong* – do you understand what I say to you?"

"Yes! yes!" Mrs. Ling said. "And I thank you for your kindness. I will talk to them again."

"That's fine, Mrs. Ling," Malpractice said. "Real fine. I'll see you later."

"Yes," the Vietnamese woman said. "*Chao ong.*"

Malpractice got to his feet and wasted no time in going over to the Command Element. He squatted down beside Falconi, leaning close to the commander and speaking low. "Sir, we got big problems with them women and kids."

"That's what I figured," Falconi replied. "Are there any fresh casualties?"

"Not physical ones, sir," Malpractice answered.

Falconi sighed. "The civilians are about to come unglued, aren't they?"

"I'm afraid so, Colonel," Malpractice said. "We gotta get 'em the hell outta here. A couple more attacks, and they're gonna jump up and try to skedaddle."

Falconi's grim silence expressed his concern.

Malpractice treated himself to a luke-warm drink from his canteen. "I wish we could evacuate 'em."

"That's not part of the agreement for this campaign," Falconi said. "So the 'Rules Committee' won't approve it."

"Hell, sir! Half of that frigging committee is a bunch of KGB pricks!" Malpractice exclaimed. "Anyhow, if we lost on account of helping out non-combatants we'd look better, wouldn't we?"

Falconi shook his head. "Not to the intelligence community, Malpractice. Potential double-agents would view our compassion as being soft in the head."

"Fuck 'em!" Malpractice snapped in anger.

"You bet," Falconi agreed. "Fuck 'em!" Falconi didn't want to mention that he'd received orders to abandon the civilians. So far, only he, Sparks Johnson and the three team leaders knew about the explicit instructions and his equally explicit refusal to obey the cruel but practical orders from Brigadier General Taggart. "We've got to figure a way to get them to safety."

"Then we'll have to take 'em ourselves, sir," Malpractice said. "Those goddamned Red Bears ain't gonna let those poor women and kids walk away from here."

Before Falconi could make any more comments, a sudden outbreak of furious fighting broke loose to the north. Malpractice instinctively lowered his head. "I gotta get back to my team, sir." He turned to leave, but stopped and looked back at his commanding officer. "I know you'll come up with the right idea. See you later.

Falconi watched Malpractice cross the perimeter. "Command is a lonely job," he said.

Archie Dobbs, sitting nearby munching on a C-ration cereal bar, looked over. "What, sir?"

"I said for you to get your butt over to the north side," Falconi snapped. He gestured to Sparks Johnson. "You too, goddamnit!"

"Aye, aye, sir!" the navy man exclaimed as he scrambled after the scout.

By then the fighting had escalated to a roaring inferno of small arms fire. Paulo Garcia and Dwayne Simpson, now with Archie and Sparks flanking them, poured a curtain of lead into the jungle ahead of them. They could see the somber camouflage uniforms of the Red Bears flitting through the jungle, drawing closer through fire and maneuver. The enemy volleys leaped in intensity, turning the air overhead into a screaming expanse, split by cracking bullets.

Swift Elk got on his radio. "Falcon! This is Eagle Two! Gimme that goddamned machine gun now! We need heavy support fast! I think the whole damned Red Bear outfit is trying to crash through here. Over."

Falconi's voice was calm and reassuring. "Wilco. Out."

In moments, Gunnar had the bore of the M60 spitting out over the Roughnecks in an enfilading pattern. It slowed up the attack some, but not much.

Archie Dobbs fired methodically and regularly.

It was at times like this that he wasn't the wild impetuous boy people saw him to be. He took clean, crisp sight pictures and squeezed off each round as if it were a separate, unattached act that was not connected with other shots he had either fired or soon would. The scout was aware of Gunnar's bullets flying overhead, but he made no conscious note of them other than to concentrate a bit on keeping his head down.

But Ray Swift Elk could not enjoy the luxury of individualistic action. He was in command, and held the responsibility for seeing to it that his side of the perimeter stood fast and strong against the growing strength of the Red Bear assault.

And the Sioux Indian officer didn't like this present situation one goddamned bit.

"Falcon!" he yelled into his radio. "This is Eagle One. I gotta have at least one more man here. Those fuckers are pressing in closer now and I can't force 'em back."

"Roger," Falconi said. "Eagle Three, send one man to Eagle One's position. Out."

Calvin Culpepper, monitoring his radio, didn't bother to answer. He just yelled over at Dean Fotopoulus. "Greek! Go help out the Roughnecks."

"Hup, Sarge!" Dean hollered back. He rolled out of his fighting hole and leaped up into a crouch to hurry over to Swift Elk's team. When he arrived, he didn't make an announcement or pass the time of day. Fotopoulus simply leaped in between Paulo and Dwayne. Within a split

197

second, his M16 had joined theirs in a chorus of blasting death.

The Red Bears advanced relentlessly through the steel hail. Major Karlov, as a Russian, felt an obligation to keep his men in the forefront of the attack. "*Zhiboy* – quickly!" he screamed at them.

His section, heeding their commander's orders, rushed forward at a reckless speed. One of them a young naval infantryman, was too anxious. Three slugs from Gunnar's machine gun stitched him across the chest and he stumbled backward under the triple punch. Blood streamed from his mouth and nose, but he recovered enough to stagger forward. But several crisscrossing M16 rounds slapped into the determined Red, spinning him around. His legs gave way and he collapsed dead to the ground.

The other two sections under Dzhurov and Deintz came up on the flanks of Karlov's men and supported them as they pushed forward. The three sections formed a rough V-shaped formation. Krashchenko, Ali Khail, and the Polish paratrooper Spichalski advanced in the hollow of the battling group. Behind them, firing from the hip, the two-man RPD machine gun crew supported it all with evenly spaced sprays of 7.62 bullets.

On the other side of the fight, Swift Elk was catching hell. His portion of the line was now outnumbered sixteen to six, and he was having the devil's time in throwing back the attack. A cool professional, he reported in to his commander via radio. "Falcon, this is Eagle One. I can't hold this sector for more than another ten minutes. Over."

"Roger, Eagle One," Falconi radioed back. "Make that fifteen minutes. Over."

Swift Elk's reply was matter-of-fact. "Wilco. Out."

Falconi didn't use the radio to contact Top's Terrors. He made a personal call on the sergeant major. He rushed across the open space and crowded into Top's fighting hole with him. Like Swift Elk, he didn't mince words. "We're making a permanent withdrawal to the south. You're leading the way with those women and children. We'll cover for you. Go!"

"Malpractice!" Top yelled out. "Salty! Blue! Get your gear and c'mon, we got work to do."

The fire team left their area bag-and-baggage to follow after their leader.

Now Falconi got on his radio to raise Swift Elk. "Eagle One. We're leaving here when that fifteen minutes is up. I'll take care of that. You come last, but put out a three-man rear guard. Over."

"That's damned near suicidal," Swift Elk communicated back. "Over."

"Do it! Out."

Swift Elk didn't waste a beat. "Dwayne, Archie, Dean! You're rear guard. Cover our asses!"

The three Black Eagles glanced around to align themselves, then went back to the deadly job at hand.

199

Chapter 17

Under First Lieutenant Swift Elk's competent orders, the Roughnecks stepped up their rate of fire to a thundering explosion of flashing primers, bursting powder and flying bullets. Yelling lustily, they swept the barrels of their rifles back and forth across the battle front.

Then they pulled back, still shooting.

Archie Dobbs, Dwayne Simpson and Dean Fotopoulus stayed. All three rifles were set for full automatic, and the volleys they sprayed criss-crossed in the continuing overlapping fields of fire.

The Red Bears to the direct front had been forced to stick their faces into the ground by the Roughnecks' furious fusillades. Their forward momentum had been brought to a complete halt, but they were now recovering with the lessening of incoming rounds. Under the bellowing orders of their section leader, the Reds moved forward against the three lone riflemen of the Black

Eagle Detachment.

Back in the rear of the American unit, Malpractice McCorckel was gathering up women and children. Making sure that the injured went first, he herded them rearward between Salty O'Rourke and Blue Richards who walked slowly backward, their weapons trained toward the shooting. If any flanking movement from the enemy hit them, that particular duo would be damned good and ready.

Top Gordon led the exodus at the head of the formation, ready for any trick from the communist foes who might try an enveloping maneuver.

Mrs. Ling, tired and worn, still held the baby. The child's mother, her condition of shock worsening, stumbled along beside the old woman in a glassy-eyed daze. The old lady sought out Malpractice. "*Bac-Si! Bac-Si!* You are not driving us away, are you?"

"Of course not, *Ba* Ling," Malpractice said. "I promise you that will not happen."

"Then where are we going?"

"Away from the bad men," Malpractice explained. "My friends will fight them up ahead while we go that way." He pointed to the south in the direction that Top Gordon led them. "When we are finally safe, we will quit running."

Mrs. Ling was no fool. Although she had never been a soldier, combat situations were something the lady had experienced in the past. She could certainly assess the circumstances to its fullest. The old woman realized completely the danger that the Americans had put themselves in. "*Bac-*

201

Si, you and your soldiers are risking your lives for us!"

Malpractice smiled softly at her. "In that case, *Ba* Ling, you are obligated to obey every order and instruction we give. It would be a shame if we sacrificed ourselves in vain, wouldn't it?"

Mrs. Ling was humbly grateful. "Of course, *Bac-Si.* Thank you—*cam on ong!*"

"*Khong co gi,*" Malpractice politely replied. "Now, please hurry along. And tell the other ladies and the older children to help out when they can."

By that time, at the front of the battle, the pressure from the Red Bear attack had built up to the point that the three-man rear guard was finally forced to begin its withdrawal. Dwayne Simpson, as the senior man, gave the orders. But there was no frantic rush for the rear. Instead, they moved with stealth—one at a time—covering each other to the maximum.

This forced the Reds pressing in on them to advance toward them cautiously. Careless or rash acts on their part, such as not hitting the dirt every few moments could get them blown away to that great collective farm in the sky.

But three people against sixteen can only do so much and the pressure kept building until an overwhelming amount of fire began pouring in on them.

Archie had just made a run rearward under Dwayne Simpson's M16 shots. The scout turned to flop down to cover Dean Fotopoulus who was farther forward. Dean leaped out, cut loose with

202

a long fireburst, and turned for a frantic race to the next bit of concealment with Archie and Dean hosing bullets past him.

Then the Greek-American stumbled.

He winced at the numbing pain in his back. Another round hit him on the right shoulder and blew away a large hunk of trapezius muscle in a crimson spray. Dean immediately went into shock. He slowly turned around to face the enemy.

"Come on! Come on!" Archie screamed. "Watch what you're doing, for Chrissake! Come back this way, Greek!"

Now the Red Bears' machine gun crew was up on their line. The gunner Ryzhyko maneuvered into position to fire his heavy automatic weapon.

"Greek!" Dwayne yelled. "Don't give it up, baby! This way! Run this way!" He looked over at Archie with a wild gesture. "Oh, man! He don't know what he's doing!"

Ryzhyko, with his buddy Grolevski minding the belt, pulled the trigger of his RPD machine gun with cold calculation.

Dean looked like he'd been kicked in the belly by a mule as he was jerked around by the impact of the heavy slugs. He fell over to one side, then rolled over on his back.

It was over.

Archie, trembling with rage, sat there until the cooler, wiser Dwayne grabbed him roughly by the shoulder. "Archie! Archie! Shake your ass!"

Archie's mind came back to reality and he leaped up to run back as fast as he could, a few steps behind Dwayne. The air around them sang with the machine gun bullets streaking through it, and spurts of dust from lower shots leaped up around their feet.

But they made it.

When the two reached the Black Eagle main line of resistance, Dwayne reported in to his team leader. "Dean didn't make it."

Those four words told the whole story.

Back behind the Red Bear formation, Krashchenko was getting worried about his machine gun team. The naval infantrymen manning the weapon were getting carried away in their battle lust. Krashchenko couldn't afford to lose them. "Ali Khail!" he called out.

The Cossack KGB sergeant, engrossed in the fighting, did not respond until he'd been called three times. Finally he noted his commanding officer's voice shouting his name in a near panic.

Ali Khail eased back from the front line, then sprinted to report in. *"Da, Tovarisch Podpolkovnik?"*

"I don't want the RPD wasted. Go get Ryzhyko and Grolevski," he said. "Then kick that damned Pole Spichalski in the ass for not maintaining some control over them."

Ali Khail wordlessly whirled around and rushed off to the task. He sprinted and dodged through Dzhurov's section until he caught up with the machine gunners. Knowing that shouting could not be heard, the Cossack simply came up behind Ryzhyko and tackled him.

Enraged, the Russian rolled over and punched

Ali Khail in the face. Ali Khail spat blood, but maintained his temper even as he grabbed the machine gunner's arms and pinned them to the ground. "*Otdeplivat,*" he hissed in anger. "Pull back! The comrade lieutenant colonel orders this! You idiots are going to get yourselves killed!"

The other man, Grolevski, pulled the Cossack off his buddy, then grabbed Ryzhyko and hauled him to his feet. "Calm down, Comrade," he urged him. "The *tovarisch serzhant* is right. We are too far forward and are risking our machine gun. Let us rejoin the *tovarisch podpolkovnik.*"

Ryzhyko, still trembling with anger, glared at Ali Khail. But he picked up the big weapon and moved rearward with Grolevski trailing him.

Ali Khail jiggled a loosened tooth with his tongue and vowed vengeance. He glared at Ryzhyko. "You have made a big mistake, comrade. You struck a Cossack in the face!"

Ryzhyko started to reply, but changed his mind. There was another job on hand. He turned away and spotted Spichalski coming toward him to join the two machine gunners. Ali Khail let the Polish paratrooper go past him, then he trotted up behind the man and kicked him hard. "That is from the Comrade Lieutenant Colonel!" Ali Khail screamed. "Tend to your duties and make sure the machine gun crew does not go beyond the front formations again!"

Properly chastised, Spichalski only treated Ali Khail to a dull look, then he continued after his partners.

Krashchenko was relieved to see that the members of his main support group were unharmed. But he had precious little time to congratulate himself or them. "Get behind Deintz's section," he ordered them. "The German is going to make a concentrated effort against the Black Eagles."

Ryzhyko affected a quick salute, then led his men off to tend to the task.

Across the battlefield, Malpractice McCorckel personally led the women and children as fast as he dared. He had taken the child from Mrs. Ling to allow the old lady to tend to the combat-shocked younger woman who now clung to her and wept piteously. Top was up at the front while Salty and Blue took care of the flanks.

By that time, Ray's Roughnecks were wearing thin. They'd taken the brunt of the fighting for the previous two hours and the strain was telling. Swift Elk's baritone voice had become hoarse while Paulo Garcia and Dwayne Simpson had begun to move around like zombies. Only Archie Dobbs, who had joined them at the front, was enthusiastic. But he was a crazy, hyper son of a bitch out in the field anyway.

Falconi lost no time in relieving them.

Calvin Culpepper's Crapshooters moved forward while the Roughnecks filtered back through them. When Doc Robichaux reached the main line of resistance, he found Archie Dobbs waiting there. "Howdy, Doc," Archie said. "The left flank is mine."

"Okay," Doc agreed. "I'll take the center and Hank is on the right."

"Gotcha," Hank Valverde called out as he moved into position.

Calvin Culpepper kept himself slightly to the rear so that he could maintain control over his small command. His combat responsibilities jumped ten-fold about a minute after he and his men were positioned.

The East German Deintz launched his section of Red Bears straight at them. This was an all-out attack without any pretense at finesse or strategy.

It was lock horns and kick ass.

The Red Bears' Fourth Section assaulted in a classic skirmish formation with their leader Deintz to the rear for control. His German-accented voice boomed out even over the shooting as he kept his men dressed on each other as they threw their own covering fire out to the front.

But Archie Dobbs had positioned himself a bit off the center of the battle area. He had a good cross-fire aim on the advancing communists. When the time was right, he fired two evenly-spaced fully automatic showers of bullets.

The center man in Deintz's unit flopped over on his belly. A damned tough Czechoslovak paratrooper, he got gamely back to his feet and lurched forward.

Now Archie was really pissed off. He pulled back on the trigger and held it until the entire contents of the twenty-round magazine was emptied.

The Czech danced and jerked under the impact of the volley. He finally staggered sideways on wobbly knees until he bumped into another man. Both went down, but only one got up.

The Czech was a butchered hunk of hamburger by then.

Archie's demonic shooting encouraged Hank Valverde and Doc Robichaux. Their combined fire from prone positions was backed by Calvin Culpepper who sent his own slugs flying over their heads.

Finally even Deintz, as fanatical as any communist military officer could be, saw he had pushed his attack effort to the maximum. A minute more in that metal hail of screaming steel, and his entire section—himself included—would be gone forever.

"Otdeplivat!" he ordered to his two survivors.

Krashchenko and his machine gun team had advanced far enough by that time to be able to accurately assess the situation. The KGB lieutenant colonel didn't want to lose the entire section at that time. He bellowed over at Ryzhyko and Golevski, "You must cover the Fourth Section with that machine gun. *Zhiboy*—quickly!"

The two naval infantrymen went into action with the speed and efficiency of a well-oiled and tuned machine. Within a very few seconds, they were sending a cover shower of heavy automatic fire over Deintz and his men.

But Krashchenko still wasn't satisfied. "Ali Khail! Spichalski! Cover the flanks of the machine gun!" He wanted no quick counter-attack to roll into them.

Archie Dobbs had attempted just that. But the quick action of the Cossack forced him back. Once again he locked eyes with the mustachioed Red Bear. Archie, screaming in rage, fired wildly as he pulled back to realign himself with Calvin, Doc, and Hank.

Calvin, satisfied that his men were coordinated once again, ordered them to withdraw. They pulled the retrograde movement as a single unit, relying on their own firepower to give them the opportunity to break contact and rejoin the main body of the Black Eagles.

A scant three minutes later, Lieutenant Colonel Falconi now had all fourteen of his men under his direct supervision. Now, with no firm plan in mind, he ordered them to continue the movement south.

Chapter 18

Chuck Fagin was summoned to Brigadier General Taggart's office in a tersely worded message that contained two main orders:

1. Come at once!
2. Come alone!

Andrea Thuy delivered the short note that had been brought to them by an MP guard. The young soldier evidently had been put under a bit of pressure too. "Tell Mister Fagin to hurry, ma'am," he said tersely but politely.

"I'll give him the word," Andrea promised. When she went into her boss' office, her face was a mask of concern. "Taggart wants to see you alone. I can't help but worry about why he doesn't want me to come with you."

Fagin shrugged. "Not to worry, my dear. You know how these old brigadier generals are. Taggart probably figures whatever he has to discuss will be more than your poor little female mind can cope with."

"Such as bad news," Andrea said.

Fagin stood up and walked around the desk. He hugged the young woman and held her tenderly. "Now, now Andrea. If it was the bad news you fear, I'm sure even that crusty old general would have the good taste to come here himself and tell you face-to-face."

"I suppose," she said unconvinced. She looked up into her friend's face. "Chuck, if it is that *bad* news, you'll go ahead and let me know right away. I'm afraid I'd lose my cool if you tried to be even the least bit considerate."

He smiled and released her. "Okay, pal. You can consider that a promise. Now I have to go." He went outside and joined the military policeman who was waiting for him.

Fagin knew something serious was in the wind when the normal security procedures were shortcut and he was almost hauled by the big MP into the elevator. "Goddamnit, hurry up, Mister Fagin," the guy urged him.

"Whoa!" Fagin said. "What's the rush?"

"I don't know," the MP said. "The old man is pissed off! And I mean to the fucking limit!"

Fagin grinned. "Better to be pissed off than pissed on, right?"

"In this case—no!" the guard said.

They stepped out of the elevator on the third floor and went down the hall to the general's quarters. The MP knocked on the door. He turned to Fagin. "Lots of luck."

Then he fled.

Fagin, puzzled, watched the young man go,

then turned and went through the door that was electronically opened from within.

Taggart was waiting for the CIA man—not behind his desk, but standing in the middle of the room with legs spread and arms folded across his chest.

"Fagin!"

"Yes, General?"

"What the hell does it take to make that god-damned Falconi obey an order?" Taggart demanded in a shout.

At times like these, Fagin could be uncharacteristically calm and cool. "Why, General. All one has to do is give him the order—"

"Bullshit!"

"—and Colonel Falconi will obey it," Fagin continued doggedly. "After all, he is a professional military man and, as such, is dedicated—"

"Shut up!" Taggart yelled.

"—to proper discipline—"

"SHUT UP!" Taggart bellowed.

"—and unquestioning obedience to—"

"*SHUT UP!*" Taggart screamed.

"Mmmm," Fagin mused aloud. "General, am I mistaken, or do I perceive a problem here?"

Taggart now began pacing back and forth. But he kept his eyes pinned on Fagin, even pointing at him from time to time. "Don't be a wiseass, Fagin! You know goddamned well that there's a problem—a goddamned big one!"

Fagin shrugged in an exaggerated way. "General Taggart, honest to God, I've not been informed of any difficulty where Colonel Falconi is concerned."

"Of course you have, you sonofabitch!" Taggart hollered. "We were discussing it the last time you were in my office."

"Oh, yeah! Now I remember. You mean his romance with Andrea Thuy, correct?" Fagin said with a smile. "I thought that was all cleared up."

The general strode across the room and stuck his face into Fagin's. "I am not goddamned talking about their goddamned stupid romance, goddamnit!" Taggart hissed. "I am talking about those civilians he has with him."

"Oh," Fagin said pleasantly.

"I have ordered him—*ordered him*—to abandon that bunch of civilians and get back to the job of kicking Krashchenko's ass," Taggart said.

"And what was his reply to that, General?"

Taggart frowned ferociously. "Goddamnit, Fagin! What do you think it was?"

"I think," Fagin said matter-of-factly, "that Falconi told you to take your orders and shove 'em up your ass."

Taggart sputtered. "That, in effect, is what he said." He began pacing again. "I'll have his tail on this one, believe me."

"No you won't."

"Yes, I will! You goddamned bet I will," Taggart said. "I'm gonna court-martial that sonofabitch and make him pull thirty years in Leavenworth. And I'll have 'em torture him every day until he gets out. Then I'll have the sonofabitch shot. And I'll tell 'em to burn his goddamned body to cinders, and throw the ashes to the wind." He glared at Fagin. "That's exactly what I'll do, goddamnit!"

"Yes, General," Fagin said calmly.

Taggart was so angry he was shaking. He went over to his liquor cabinet and pulled out a glass. Next he grabbed a bottle. After starting to pour, he hit the tumbler so hard that it flew across the room. The general tipped up the bottle and took a half dozen deep swallows. Then he slammed it down and had a coughing fit that turned his face purple.

Fagin became a bit concerned. "Jesus! Are you okay, General?"

It took Taggart a full two minutes to recover. Finally he wheezed, "Uh, uh, yeah. I'm fine." He swallowed. "Okay, Fagin, I need your help."

Fagin shook his head. "Hold everything! I'm not helping with this one."

Taggart sneered. "Oh my! Don't tell me an agency spook like you is a bleeding heart when it comes to women and kids. Even if they affect the outcome of an operation."

"Look, General, Falconi is going to do exactly what he thinks is right," Fagin calmly explained. "He won't obey you, and he won't obey the Central Intelligence Agency if he considers any orders illegal or immoral. All we can do is hope things work out okay."

"How can they, Fagin? He's got a handpicked, hardcore cadre of highly motivated Red killers on his ass. Falconi is hampered by trying to protect a bunch of women and kids. He can't attack, counterattack or defend himself properly under those circumstances. What the hell is he going to do?"

"One of two things, General," Fagin answered. "Win or die." He paused. "Is there anything else?"

"I expected a hell of a better reaction than that from you, Fagin," Taggart said.

"Sorry."

Taggart sighed. "Get outta here."

"Goodbye, General." Fagin went outside the office and returned down to his own place with the same MP guard.

The MP was impressed. "You really got the general pissed off. I could hear him yelling at you."

Fagin shrugged. "What's the big deal about that?"

"The general's office is soundproof, Mister Fagin!"

Krashchenko kicked at the sprawled body of the Black Eagle Dean Fotopoulous. "This one really got shot up," he remarked to Ali Khail.

"He was a part of that group that slowed down our initial assault," Ali Khail said. "Ryzhyko caught him straight on with the RPD machine gun."

"Good shooting," Krashchenko said. He turned to look across the clearing as the Red Bears wrapped up the body of one of his own men. This was the Czechoslovakian paratrooper. They used the man's own poncho as a shroud. "He died fighting," he said to Ali Khail beside him. "I saw

215

him go down."

"I witnessed his death as well, *Tovarisch Pod-polkovnik,*" Ali Khail said in open admiration. "He took several bursts of full automatic fire."

A shallow grave had already been dug, and the man's comrades tenderly placed him in it. They quickly gathered around the shallow excavation. The burial was completed without any ceremony other than a quick statement by Krashchenko:

"He died for the glory of world socialism," the lieutenant colonel said. "We should be proud of his memory and hold it in our hearts forever." Thus, the funeral service ended as fast as it began. "I want to see all section leaders in five minutes. Set up a temporary defense perimeter in the meantime. We will not be here long."

The task was accomplished in the allotted time, and Krashchenko had situated himself off to one side with his ranking officers. "We have lost two men," he said.

The Russian Major Karlov responded. "And so have the Black Eagles, Comrade Lieutenant Colonel," he reminded him. "We are even, *nyet?*"

"*Nyet!*" Krashchenko answered. "We should have done much better because Falconi has burdened himself with those villagers. There is no doubt that he is attempting to escort them out of harm's way."

"They will hinder him," Dzhurov said. "Surely, the American will eventually abandon those people."

Krashchenko shook his head. "No, I am convinced he won't. I know that idiot Falconi. He is

216

soft in the head and heart. Although forced to travel slowly, he will continue on this stupid quest."

"We can move twice—even three times faster than him," Deintz said.

"Of course," Krashchenko said. "So what do you think we should do?"

"Catch the Black Eagles and kill all of them," Karlov said.

"That is exactly what we will do, *Tovarisch Mayor*," Krashchenko said. "And I will reward the men by giving the women to them. But reaching that point won't be easy. Haven't we just learned that all-out frontal attacks are costly?"

"Yes," Dzhurov said. "I must admit that Falconi and his men are skilled fighters in this jungle. Therefore, I respectfully suggest that we should try hit-and-run probes until we wear the Black Eagles down."

"That is exactly what we are going to do," Krashchenko said. "Each time we attack, we stay just long enough to kill a Black Eagle. Then we pull back and wait for the next opportunity. The beauty of these tactics is that we can pick and choose when we want to fight. The Black Eagles will be forced to play a losing, defensive hand without any trump cards."

"When do we start?" Deintz asked.

"Now!" Krashchenko barked. "Form up your sections. We leave now to search out the Black Eagles and kill the first man in their self-made chain of death!"

* * *

An extra heavy load of wounded had come into Long Binh that particular day. Men of the 1st Cav had made a helicopter-borne assault into a number of hot landing zones that had nearly ended in disaster.

Only the tenacity and bravery of the small unit commanders at the squad and platoon level had staved off a complete massacre. But there had been an unusually heavy load of casualties to take care of by the hard-pressed medical personnel back in the rear.

Normally, Betty Lou Pemberton and her friend Jean McCorckel worked the convalescent ward where recovering victims of the fighting were rested up and prepared for eventual transport back to the States. But because of the sudden influx of stretchers from the 1st Cav, the two were called over to the surgical tent to act as prep nurses for the necessary operations to save the brave shot-up troopers.

The work lasted from early morning to late that evening. By the time the last patients were finally carried in for the exhausted surgeons' attention, both young nurses were ready to call it a day.

So tired they didn't speak, they walked out of the hospital quonset hut and walked through the gate. Suddenly Betty Lou grabbed Jean's hand and stopped. "Look!"

Andrea Thuy pulled up in a jeep and waved cheerfully at them. "I was over at the nurse's quarters and the charge of quarters told you two were pulling an extra shift with one of the surgical units."

Betty Lou was relieved to see how peppy Andrea was. "I was scared to death when I first saw you."

"Hey," Andrea said. "Nothing is wrong. Come on, you two. Hop in. I'll take you over to your billets for hot showers and a change of clothing. Then dinner is on me at the officer's club."

The two nurses got into the vehicle and Andrea gunned the engine and drove off. She glanced over and winked. Despite her outward optimism and lighthearted conduct, Andrea was worried sick inside. Chuck Fagin had given her the full story of what Falconi was trying to pull off in the mission area. They had discussed the situation fully, and made a cold blooded analysis of the chances of the Black Eagles coming out of the operation.

It looked like a hundred-to-one against survival.

Betty Lou, in the back seat, leaned forward so Andrea could hear her. "What's the latest news from the boys?"

Andrea forced a smile. "Everything is sailing along."

Betty Lou nodded and leaned back in the small seat. The rush of wind across her face felt good. She closed her eyes and enjoyed the sensation.

Andrea drove on, her teeth clenched tightly together.

Chapter 19

The Black Eagles' rate of travel was painfully slow. A combined problem of heavy vegetation and the extra burden of the Vietnamese women and children caused them to move at a slow walk.

This situation was so dangerous that they had become the proverbial sitting ducks.

To add to the problem, noise discipline was almost completely out of the question. The children, frightened and hungry, continually cried and sobbed aloud. Now and then one would call out loudly for a father now lying dead from the Red Bears' execution. The mothers did their best to comfort the little ones, but some of the women, close to cracking after all the hell they had endured, could barely control their own fear and emotions.

Due to the sluggish speed, the center of the column was a relatively easy place to be for the members of the Black Eagle Detachment. Because the team pulling duty at the front was charged with clearing away the vegetation, those following immediately behind had the luxury of being able to squat down and rest every few minutes. The work with the machetes in that steamy heat, however, was exhausting and the men wielding them had to be spared after every quarter of an hour. The tired individual, soaked in energy-sapping sweat, would stagger back to the rear of his team and gratefully sink to the ground for a few blessed moments of rest while the next guy fatigued himself to the ultimate in the performance of this necessary but painful chore.

The situation wasn't much better on the flanks. Because of the ease the enemy would have in hitting them, the Black Eagles couldn't relax their guard enough to clear the jungle in their path. The flankers had to move directly through the brush and vines that scratched and scraped their exposed skin.

This was the duty of Top's Terrors just before noon on the first day of the journey toward safety. Malpractice was to the front, Blue Richards brought up the rear, while Salty O'Rourke covered the center of the left flank.

Top moved around from man-to-man so he could keep an accurate and up-to-date assessment of the situation. It was a good way to give the exhausted men a bit of encouragement and keep their spirits up. This was also necessary because Falconi kept his radio buzzing as he continually checked in with the team leaders for support.

"Eagle Two, this is Falcon. Over."

Top turned to his Prick-Six radio. "This is Eagle Two. Over."

"How goes the war, Eagle Two? Over."

Top grinned and replied. "To hell with it. We're pulling R&R on the right flank. Over."

"Roger," came back Falconi's voice. The amusement was not hidden in it. "If you find any goodlooking women, you're instructed to raise me immediately. Out."

Salty O'Rourke, a few paces away, had heard the exchange. He looked back and grinned at Top. "I'm the closest thing you got to a pretty girl, you poor dumb bastard."

Top started to laugh, but the jungle suddenly exploded with heavy automatic fire. Top's Terrors immediately reacted with return shooting. Salty O'Rourke, responsible for the center of the flank, ran forward to make sure that Malpractice and Blue weren't caught too far out of alignment.

His devotion to duty caused him to catch two machine gun slugs in the chest.

The incoming rounds suddenly ceased. The attackers could easily be heard rapidly withdrawing through the brush. Then the jungle was deathly quiet. After a minute's wait, the team pulled in closer together.

Top crawled over to Salty. "Hey, marine."

Salty was lying on his back. His face was as white as the belt on his dress blues. He grinned with blood stuck to his teeth. "Hey, dogface."

"Just a minute. Let Malpractice have a look at

you," Top said.

Salty was a veteran. As such he had already judged the extent of his wounds. "Tell that ol' boy to forget it."

"Knock off the shit," Top said.

Malpractice already had his aid kit out as he knelt down beside Salty. He immediately loosened the man's web gear and opened his fatigue jacket. Salty's chest was a mass of blood, and there was one hole the size of a man's fist that showed some pink lung.

Salty started wheezing. "Sucking—chest—wound," he announced to Malpractice.

Malpractice frowned. "Hey, marine. I'm the medic. I can recognize the type of wound you're going to use to goof off in the hospital with."

"I've—I've—had it," Salty said.

"Bullshit. Like I said, I'm the medic," Malpractice said working frantically with a dressing to stuff up the hole. "Nobody is allowed to cork off here without written permission from Colonel Falconi. So you'll be around so long the fucking marine corps is gonna be forced to make you a gunnery sergeant whether you deserve the promotion or not."

"I'll—never—be—be a gunny," Salty said. His mouth dropped open and stayed that way, with his eyes rolled upward. He was still.

"Salty's dead," Malpractice said.

Falconi and Archie Dobbs arrived on the scene. Falconi knelt beside Salty's corpse. He reached over and gently closed the dead man's eyes. "The marines always send us good men,"

Falconi said.

"That's because they ain't got any bad'uns, sir," Archie said.

"I agree," Malpractice said. "He's the fourth gyrene to die with us."

"The sixth," Archie said. "If you count Chun and Park. Two Korean marines and four American marines—that's six."

Falconi stood up. "Let's go. Archie get back up at the front. Top, cover the rear. I'm going to put Calvin's people out here for awhile."

"Yes, sir," Top said.

The war went on.

Ali Khail, with the machine gun crew behind him, reported in to Krashchenko. "*Tovarisch Podpolkovnik*, our ambush was a success. We hit them hard and fast. After one man went down, we quickly broke contact and withdrew. The Black Eagle return fire did us no damage."

"*Koroschi*—excellent!" Krashchenko said. "Within a couple of days we will have Falconi and his men going insane with anxiety and rage. They will never know when or where we will hit them. As long as they are anchored down with those children, they will be at our mercy. We shall kill them at our leisure." He looked over at his machine gunner. "Ryzhyko, you have done well."

Ryzhyko said nothing. He looked from Krashchenko to Ali Khail, then back again. "Am I dismissed, Comrade Lieutenant Colonel?"

"Of course," Krashchenko said. He watched the machine gunner leave with his ammunition bearer. "Ali Khail, is there bad blood between you and Ryzhyko?"

"He struck me in the face," Ali Khail. "That is a supreme insult to a Cossack!"

Krashchenko snarled at him. "You ceased being a Cossack when you became a soldier of socialism. Ethnic eccentricities are not tolerated by Mother Russia."

"That is only true when the man involved is a European Russian," Ali Khail said.

Krashchenko's eyes narrowed with anger. "Are you being insolent, *Tovarisch Serzhant?* It would not be wise for even a decorated KGB border guard like yourself to accuse the central communist party of racist leanings. Is that what you wish to do?"

Ali Khail snapped to attention and saluted. "*Nyet, Tovarisch Podpolkovnik.*"

"I will not tolerate insubordination or treasonous remarks. Is that understood?"

Ali Khail nodded. "Yes," Comrade Lieutenant Colonel."

"Now send me Deintz. It is time for his squad to play at nipping Falconi's flanks."

Calvin Culpepper, with an OD-colored bandanna wrapped around his head, motioned his team forward. "Let's go, Crapshooters. We got the honor of breaking trail for awhile."

"I'm better at breaking wind," Hank Valverde

said with a grin. Then he did exactly that.

"Whew!" Calvin sniffed. "Goddamn, boy! I think something crawled up your ass and died."

"Aw, that was nothing," Hank said modestly. "You should smell my farts after I been eating jalapeno peppers."

Doc Robichaux, wincing behind him, gave the Chicano a friendly shove. "The Geneva Convention absolutely forbids gas warfare. They'd make you go home."

Hank farted again. "San Antonio, here I come!"

"Forget San Antonio, and get that damned machete swinging," Calvin said.

"*Por su puesto*, Sergeant," Hank said grinning. He pulled out the cutting instrument and got to work with hard, efficient, rhythmic swings. "My grandpa down in Sinaloa made his living doing this to sugar cane. It's an inherited talent in the Valverde family."

Chop! Chop! Chop!

Doc settled in behind him, swinging his gaze back and forth across the front. His rifle was fully locked and loaded, the selector put on full auto. The idea of this was to be able to throw out any covering fire for Hank to pull back under in case of a sudden attack.

But it didn't work.

A wild-eyed mustachioed figure suddenly rose up to their direct front and fired a short burst of AK-47 fire before ducking down.

Hank flipped over on his back, and Doc threw out a full magazine, then rushed forward. He

226

searched frantically around for a corpse or for evidence of a wounded man crawling away. He found nothing. Not even a spot of blood. He spat out a couple of damned good Cajun cuss words, then turned around and went back to the team.

Calvin knelt beside Hank. He looked up as Doc approached. "He's gone, man."

Doc, a navy seal corpsman, knew death when he saw it. Hank Valverde, his eyelids half closed and a blank expression on his face was a classic corpse. But Doc, hoping like hell he was mistaken, dropped down for an examination. It didn't take but a couple of moments. "Shit!"

"I liked ol' Hank," Calvin said. "This was his fifth trip out with us."

Falconi and Archie Dobbs came up. "Oh, Jesus," Archie said. "We've lost Hank."

"Best supply man I ever knowed," Calvin said. "He was good to us, man. You guys remember all them nice things he brought along to put in the bunker?"

"Get his ammo," Falconi said. He laid a hand on Calvin's shoulder. "I'm sending Sparks up to join your team."

Calvin stood up and looked into his commanding officer's face. "Is this the way it goes down, sir? Are we gonna die one at a time, taking it all and not giving nothing back?"

Falconi was silent. He got a pack of cigarettes out of his pocket and took one after giving another to Calvin. "It's been rougher than this before."

"Yes, sir," Calvin agreed. "But we was always

227

able to take a few of the bastards out with us."

"We've got to keep moving," Falconi said doggedly. He turned to Archie. "Go get Sparks and tell him he's in the Crapshooters for the rest of the mission." He swept his cold gaze back to Calvin. "Move out."

"Yes, sir." He started to take out his machete.

"You're the team leader," Falconi said. "I want you to be in control here. You can't do that if you're chopping wood."

"I don't like setting somebody up," Calvin said in a cold voice.

"You're the team leader," Falconi repeated.

Before any other conversation could take place, Doc Robichaux pulled out his own blade and began attacking the jungle at the exact place Hank had died.

Calvin nodded, then he forced a grin. "What's that you're always saying, sir? Nobody said this job was gonna be easy."

"That's what I say," Falconi said. "Over and over."

Sparks Johnson broke through the brush around them and stepped forward. "Archie told me to report to you, sir."

"Not to me," Falconi said. He pointed to Calvin Culpepper. "There's your new team leader."

"Aye, aye, sir," Sparks said. Then he noticed Hank lying dead on the ground. He walked up to Calvin. "Full or semi-automatic?"

"Full auto. If something goes wrong, I want more bullets out there than flies on a dead cat's ass." Calvin said.

"You got it," Sparks said.

"Cover ol' Doc up there," Calvin continued. "After fifteen minutes you can spell him." He glanced around with a nervous movement of his head. "Let's get the hell outta here."

"If we can," Sparks said moving off to join Doc.

Chapter 20

Calvin and his two men spent another hour up at the front of the column.

Nothing spectacular happened. More energy was used up, a couple of more gallons of sweat was soaked up in their tiger fatigues, and a scant fifty meters of distance was covered through the thick monsoon forest.

The three exhausted men passed Ray's Roughnecks who had gone forward to relieve them. Paulo Garcia winked at Sparks Johnson. "Hey, did you swabs leave any jungle for us to cut away?"

Sparks, his face filthy except where heavy rivulets of sweat streaked through the dirt, forced himself to grin. "We cut our way clear to Kansas City, then figgered you guys might want something to do. So we replanted it all."

Dwayne Simpson joined in the joking. "Hey, thanks a lot! We was afraid there wouldn't be nothing to do."

Ray Swift Elk growled. "I hope you assholes are as energetic about chopping with those machetes as you are about bullshitting each other."

In sticking with the newly developed custom, the team that had been leading the way was placed in the easiest position in the middle of the column. The trio of Calvin Culpepper, Doc Robichaux, and Sparks Johnson gratefully settled down to wait while the Roughnecks slashed away enough of the brush to allow another advance.

By then even the indefatigable Archie Dobbs had begun to tire. The hours of running on nerve and adrenaline were beginning to take their toll to the extent that Falconi noticed it.

"Archie."

Dull-eyed, the scout slowly swung his gaze to the detachment commander. "Yes, sir."

"You hang in here with the Crapshooters for awhile."

"Okay, sir." Archie moved into the center position.

Doc Robichaux joined the scout and the two shared a cigarette now that smokes were beginning to become scarce within the detachment. Archie took a drag and passed the fag over to his friend. "It was really unexpected about the guys we've lost, wasn't it? I don't think anybody considered we'd take heavy casualties on this trip out."

"Yeah," Doc agreed. "I should feel bad, but I keep getting that same old selfish feeling."

"I know what you mean," Archie said. "You're glad it wasn't you."

"That's right."

"It's natural to feel that way," Archie said. "All guys in combat have that in common."

"I got another feeling though," Doc said. "And it's pure anger. There's one o' them goddamned Red Bears I'm gonna blow away."

"Me too," Archie said. "The sonofabitch I'm after has a big ol' mustache."

Doc snapped his head around so quick that his neck cracked. "That's the motherfucker that killed Hank."

"So we're both after him, huh?" Archie mused. "I'll tell you what, Doc. I got a hunnerd bucks that say I'm the one who gets him."

"You're on, Arch," Doc said. "I got a special interest in blowing that bastard and his to hell. I owe Hank at least that much."

The Red Bear section leaders were seated on the ground in a clearing. Krashchenko paced back and forth in front of them. Ali Khail, aloof and detached, stood off to one side leaning against a tree.

Finally Krashchenko turned to his subordinate leaders. "Listen carefully to what I have to say. I have reached a decision. We will change our hit-and-run tactics and make one big effort. If such an attack appears that we are able to destroy Falconi and his men, we will continue. If not, I will order a withdrawal."

"What is the plan of attack, *Tovarisch Podpolkovnik*?" Major Karlov asked.

"We will hit one side only," Krashchenko said. "With all our superior fire power concentrated on a single flank, we should be able to break through to the center of Falconi's happy little family."

Ali Khail spat. "Whichever of Falconi's men is on that side, will be wiped out to the man. I have seen them several times, Comrade Lieutenant Colonel," the Cossack said. "There will be no problem in a penetration. But we will have to fight hard to retain any advantage we gain. However, that can be easier done now than before. After all, we number fifteen to their thirteen."

Deintz, the East German, was excited. "In this kind of warfare where several trees can divide a battlefield, that is almost similar to three-to-one odds."

The Bulgarian Dzhurov had another optimistic note to add to the discussion. "Remember, comrades, when we wipe out that flank, we will kill three or four more of them. That means we will outnumber them fifteen to ten."

"Five-to-one odds using Comrade Senior Lieutenant Deintz's theory," Krashchenko said.

"The Teutonic mind is deadly logical and accurate," Deintz said immodestly. "There is not even room for errors in my calculations."

"Very well!" Krashchenko said. "Why delay Falconi's destruction? Prepare your sections for the attack." He motioned to Ali Khail. "Send the machine gun crew to me. I have special instructions for them."

The column came to a halt as some particularly thick jungle growth appeared in the direction of travel. Falconi emitted a low whistle to Top. "Relieve Ray's guys up at the front."

"Yes, sir," Top said. "C'mon, Malpractice, Blue. Let's go."

Falconi waved over at Calvin Culpepper. "Okay, Calvin. The right flank is all yours now."

"Right, sir."

Archie, feeling good himself, waved over at the commanding officer. "Can I go up with Top's guys, sir?"

"You still need to cool it for awhile," Falconi replied. "Stay where you are."

Meanwhile, Calvin, Doc Robichaux and Sparks Johnson were now almost completely recovered from the hard labor they'd done before the Roughnecks had taken their place. They moved out to flanker duty, their steps lighter and faster.

The women and children had quieted a bit by then. The sudden burst of fire that killed Hank Valverde had increased their anxiety and, consequently, their agitation. But eventually the outburst of screams and weeping eased off, until only a muffled sob could be heard coming from their group.

The jungle, too, seemed to have settled down to match the mood. It was almost as if it accepted the fact that an explosive, violent outburst would occur now and then, and there was absolutely nothing that could be done about it.

This quiet went on for a half hour.

Then the Soviet RPD machine gun blasted into action on the right flank.

Sparks Johnson's head split open from a heavy round that slammed almost directly between his eyes. The navy radio operator collapsed so fast to the ground that his grip on the M16 was still tight in death.

Calvin's rage roared up from his psyche. "The motherfuckers are always hitting me!" he bellowed. Without wasting another second, he emptied a magazine toward the enemy. "Move back to the column, Doc!"

The two withdrew from the pressing attack side-by-side. There was no time for fancy maneuvering, the duo simply stumbled backward trying vainly to exchange bullet for bullet with the Red Bears who charged them. It was too much.

Suddenly Doc bent over at the middle. "Oh, shit!"

"You hit, Doc?" Calvin cried out. He fired with one hand and moved over to his limping man.

"I got a gunshot," Doc said.

"Hang on to me, hear?" Calvin continued his one-handed effort, sniping at targets of opportunity that appeared only momentarily through the jungle greenery. Doc sagged heavier on him. "Keep moving! Keep moving!"

Doc went down on his knees. He looked up at his team leader almost apologetically. "Internal—bleeding."

"Get up, Doc. Goddamnit! We can reach the main column in another minute."

But Doc couldn't move. He took a couple of deep breaths, then pitched forward on his face.

"*You motherfuckers!*" Calvin screamed. Again he held back on his trigger until the magazine emptied. He was rewarded by seeing two of the Red Bears dumped to the ground.

Falconi and Archie appeared at his side. Falconi grabbed Calvin's sleeve. "We got covering fire from Gunnar and Tiny. Get back there."

"Get Doc, he's down!" Calvin said with tears streaming down his face.

Archie, firing, shook his head. "Doc's dead."

Calvin struggled against Falconi's grip. "No he ain't! Get up, Doc! Get up, you crazy Cajun sonofabitch!"

Archie jumped up and ran back, grabbing Calvin's other arm. "It's no use, Calvin!"

Falconi and the scout dragged the team leader toward the main column under the covering fire thrown out by Gunnar Olson. Unfortunately, there was a hell of a lot more flying bullets heading inward than outward.

The three finally were able to throw themselves to the ground beside the machine gun. Gunnar Olson, a journeyman machine gunner, worked calmly and efficiently. Instinctively measured firebursts flew outward as his trigger finger tapped out a death's tune. The length and intensity of these showers of bullets were quickly determined by instantaneous sightings on scurrying targets.

Tiny worked the ammo belts, expertly inserting a new one when necessary. The big kid had a near serene expression on his face. The noise, the shouting and the roaring of weapons meant nothing to him. His entire being was concentrated on the end of each belt and the receiver of the M60.

The Red Bears, shouting in triumph, pressed forward. They leaped from cover to cover, always drawing closer. Expertly covering each other, their storming tactics worked wonderfully for them. It seemed only a matter of time before they would sweep over the small group of Black Eagles trying to hold out against the growing strength of their assault.

Falconi's quick mind suddenly grasped the situation. He now fully understood the enemy's tactics. He hit the transmit button on his Prick-Six. "Eagle One! Eagle Two! Move to the center of the column, and come in fighting. Out!"

Ray Swift Elk's Roughnecks arrived on the scene first. They went to the right of the Black Eagle's impromptu line of defense and hit the dirt. Their three M16s added to the chorus of death being sung out to the Red Bears.

Gunnar sensed a violent movement beside him. He took his eye from the machine gun sight and glanced to his left. Tiny Burke, his eyes open in death, had rolled over on his back. A bullet had punched through his nose, smashing it in.

Gunnar had no time for grief. "Gimme an ammo bearer!" he shouted.

Archie Dobbs, the closest man, crawled over and pushed Tiny's big corpse out of the way. He grabbed the belt of ammo and steadied it while Gunnar renewed his shooting.

Now Top's Terrors arrived on the scene. They took the extreme right. Accidentally, but beautifully, the Black Eagle position had evolved into a near semi-circle.

And the Red Bears had charged into the center.

The heavy cross-fire caught the Russian Major Karlov's team heavily. They hesitated, then Karlov was suddenly whirled completely around and smashed to the ground by a volley of Black Eagle bullets.

Deintz brought his men forward to shore up the attack. But all he saw was Karlov die. He ordered his men to the ground, and they used the stationary positions to lay down a base of fire that might be the decisive factor in the explosive battle.

Dzhurov brought his section up to exploit the fire support. With the RPD machine gun crew backing them up, they stood a good chance of breaching the Black Eagle line.

But now Falconi's men had gone mad with rage. Bellowing and shooting, they increased their efforts to the point that even Deintz's well-directed fusillades began to fail.

"Black Eagles!" Falconi yelled. "Get 'em!"

The counter-attack, mounted when there never should have been one, caught the Red Bears by surprise. Dzhurov's men would have stayed there and died, but the Bulgarian wasn't about to waste them at that point.

"Otdeplivat!" he ordered. "Pull back!"

That left Deintz with no choice but to follow

238

suit. He issued his orders, and his men fired a final volley.

The Black Eagles charged into the void, then the RPD supporting fire swept across them.

Dwayne Simpson took three simultaneous hits from the 7.62-millimeter slugs and died.

But in the rear of the Red Bear formation, Lieutenant Colonel Krashchenko knew that his idea of one big attack had failed. He ordered an immediate retreat.

Contact between the opposing forces was quickly broken and, suddenly, the jungle screamed in silence.

Chapter 21

The Black Eagles threw out an extremely thin defensive perimeter after the battle. The Vietnamese women and children, now thoroughly combat-shocked, sat dully in the center. Now, for a change, there wasn't a sound from the stunned, frightened crowd.

Falconi sat with his two remaining team leaders. Calvin Culpepper, because of the loss of all his men, had been reassigned to Ray Swift Elk as a rifleman.

"We were hit hard," Falconi said to Ray and Top. "But we weren't shellacked despite losing four men in that last firefight. We hit 'em back hard and made 'em run."

Top pulled a fresh stogie—his last—from a pocket and bit off the end. "That encourages me, sir."

Swift Elk nodded. "Me too. It might have ended up a standoff, but we knocked off a couple of their people too. I'd say we're even."

"There's something else I've figured out," Falconi added. "They won't be bothering our guests."

"The women and kids?" Top asked.

"Right," Falconi answered. "That son of a bitch Krashchenko can't waste time or ammo on 'em now. He's got to come back and get us, and finish the job."

"You sound optimistic—for the Red Bears," Swift Elk growled.

"Under normal circumstances, this would be his ball game," Falconi said. "Hell, the commie son of a bitch could kick apart any defense we set up and there wouldn't be a goddamned thing we could do about it."

Malpractice McCorckel, with Mrs. Ling beside him, walked up to the command group. "I fetched the old lady like you wanted, sir."

Falconi smiled at the woman. *"Chao ba,"* Falconi said. He indicated a spot beside him. *"Ba ngoi day."*

Mrs. Ling sat down as she had been invited. The strain of the previous days showed plainly in her face, but the brave lady still managed to keep her dignity. She bowed her head to each of the men present. *"Chao ong."*

"Ba Ling," Falconi said. "It is now safe for you and the other women to take the children and travel without our escort."

"I am not sure where to take them, *Trung-Ta,"* Mrs. Ling said. "You spoke to me of a special place."

"It is to the east, in the direction in which the

241

sun rises," Falconi said. "If you go in that path you should reach an area where there are many government hamlets where you could live away from the war."

Mrs. Ling was a pragmatic woman. "And how long would we walk, *Trung-Ta?*"

"With the little ones, three days," Falconi said. "And I think you should leave now."

"Of course" Mrs. Ling said. But she was silent for several moments. "The bad men will not bother us, because they must concentrate on killing you and your men, *Trung-Ta.*"

"Yes," Falconi answered. "You are a very observant woman."

"What I have seen gave me no joy. You killed some of their men, but they killed more of yours," Mrs. Ling said. "It was not because you were a bad war leader who made poor decisions. Rather you sacrificed to save us."

"It is our way," Falconi stated.

Mrs. Ling stood up. "You will die here, *Trung-Ta.* But do not weep. The gods of the forest have seen your nobility. You and your men will be well rewarded in the afterlife after you have crossed over through the great void of death. Perhaps you will live forever as a spirit in one of the great trees. People will come to you and pray for blessings and good luck."

"*Cam on ba,*" Falconi said, not really thrilled with that particular prospect.

The Vietnamese lady waved at them. "*Chao ong.*" Then she turned and walked away.

Top took a languid draw off his stogie. "The

lady's right. We've had it."

"We're outnumbered, outgunned, stretched too thin, and cut off," Swift Elk added.

"As a matter of fact," Falconi said. "We're doomed."

"Well, sir," the sergeant major said. "In that case, what's your plan of action?"

Falconi didn't hesitate. "Hell, we attack!"

Chapter 22

Archie, his M16 at high port, moved slowly through the heavy growth. Each step, each breath, each movement of his body was a separate, conscious effort in which silence was of the utmost importance.

The scout was back in his element. He led the way with the surviving eight Black Eagles behind him. Archie followed the tracks left by the withdrawing Red Bears. This final effort, a desperate spasm of offensive warfare, could very well be the last for the detachment.

This was for the whole pie for nothing.

And timing played an important role. They had to catch the commies before they began their own offensive movement. If Krashchenko and his sons of bitches didn't have their pants down when the Black Eagles caught up with them, then the mission was a complete wipe-out.

Archie reached a large *rung* tree. He moved close to the trunk, and eased around it.

Then he bumped face-to-face with the mustachioed motherfucker he'd been looking for since this particular war had begun.

Ali Khail, his AK47 leaning up against a nearby tree, was just finishing taking a leak and had slipped his large circumcised member back into his pants. The muscular Cossack thought fast, however, and slapped out blindly but instinctively.

Now Archie stood with bare hands as his M16 spun off into the nearby brush. It was his turn to do something without thinking, and the unconscious reflex resulted in him standing there with his sharp, heavy K-Bar knife held tightly in his right fist.

Archie lunged forward and took a wide swipe.

Ali Khail, nimble as ever, danced back out of the way and brought out his own fighting blade. He got into a semi-crouch and moved slowly around.

Archie, facing him, was as alert as a cat. He noted the red bear insignia over the man's jacket pocket as both men felt each other out.

Ali Khail suddenly launched an explosive attack, but Archie leaped to the side and reached out with his free hand. He locked it tight on the Red Bear's wrist and attempted to use the man's momentum to pull him down.

But Ali Khail twisted his arm upward and pulled free.

Once again the two combatants, saying nothing, breathed heavily and warily went around in a slow circle, waiting for an opening.

The Crossack tried again. But his blade cut nothing but empty air. Archie recovered from his dodging maneuvers, and went back to the deadly waiting game.

A full minute passed, then Archie feinted a high slash, then rolled his hand and tried for a belly cut.

Ali Khail brought his blade down and it cut into the Black Eagle's forearm.

Archie grunted, feeling burning pain and the hot sticky blood flow from the cut down to his hand.

The Red Bear was encouraged. He now made quicker movements, bobbing his head and doing a boxer-like shuffle. He grinned, his teeth showing yellow under the big mustache.

Archie, wishing like hell his wound would stop throbbing, also picked up the tempo of their dance of death.

The Cossack now slipped both hands behind him to hide which held his cutting weapon. It was as much as taunt as a tactic.

Archie, also assumed a two-handed grip, but his knife was in sight in front of him. As he moved, he closely resembled a tennis player waiting for his opponent to serve the ball.

Ali Khail's attack was instantaneous.

He leaped forward and thrust toward a spot under Archie's ribs. The blade cut into Archie's fatigue jacket as the American leaped backward.

Archie sliced horizontally, and his knife bit into Ali Khail's face, slicing deeply as it slid across his eyes, cutting through the lids.

246

It looked like the Cossack's eyeballs melted as they slid out of their sockets.

Archie moved in, making two simultaneous motions. One hand gripped Ali Khail's weapon wielding arm, and the other drove the blade into the man's belly. It was quickly withdrawn and swiped across and deeply into the Red Bear's neck.

The Cossack, his face a mask of blood, and his mouth hideously opened and vomiting red bile and gore, dropped his knife and walked backward a few wobbling steps. He sat down and bowed his head as his life drained down his jacket front.

Then he toppled over.

Archie gripped his injured arm, then suddenly turned toward the crash of brush to his left.

Several more of the Red Bears, stunned at seeing him, burst into the area. They stopped in shock. Their leader, Dzhurov, reacted quickly.

"*Streliba*—fire!" he screamed.

The clearing exploded with blasting weapons.

Chapter 23

Archie wisely hit the dirt as the bullets flew over him and slapped into the Red Bear section across the clearing.

Dzhurov spun around by the impact of a bullet, faced the rear, and was stitched up the back by three more slugs that sent him reeling into the nearby brush.

The two men with him went down like sliced cornstalks.

Falconi, his M16 on full auto, stepped into the small glen with Gunnar the Gunner Olson beside him. "As they say in the movies," Falconi remarked. "We seemed to have arrived in the nick of time."

The other two teams arrived, the six men spread out in a tight skirmish position.

Archie, feeling weak now, rolled over on his back. "I need a medic."

Malpractice detached himself from Top's Terrors, and knelt beside his old buddy to administer medical aid.

Falconi had other things on his mind. "The rest of those bastards have got to be through there," he said pointing directly ahead into the tangle of jungle growth.

"We don't know what we're going to find on the other side," Top said.

Falconi shrugged. "There's only one way to find out. Move out!"

Maintaining their combat formation, the two teams damned noise discipline and charged into the heavy brush.

On the far side of the thick grove, Ryzhyko and Grolevski, the two Russian naval infantrymen, looked at each other in confusion. First Ali Khail had disappeared into the jungle, then Captain Dzhurov had taken his section in after him. Now it sounded like they were all running like hell straight back toward them.

The Polish paratrooper Spichalski, a patient man, squatted down to wait.

The first Black Eagle through the trees was Gunnar the Gunner. His eyes drank in the picture of the two men with the machine gun. The Norwegian-American recognized his ace rivals immediately, and all the battle-fury of his Viking ancestors boiled up from the depths of his soul.

The M60 machine gun rocked-and-rolled in his hands.

Ryzhyko and Grolevski turned to chopped *myaso* and bounced off each other in their death throes as they were kicked to the ground by Gunnar's flying slugs.

Spichalski was flipped over on his back in a very undignified way—but he really didn't care. The son of a bitch was as dead as boiled *khabaza* at a wedding party.

Now Ray's Roughnecks and Top's Terrors continued forward, their interlacing fire sweeping out ahead of them.

KGB Lieutenant Colonel Krashchenko and Senior Lieutenant Deintz of the East German Army quickly organized themselves and the three surviving Red Bears into a defensive formation as they pulled back into the jungle opposite from the direction of the Black Eagle attack.

Falconi reacted just as quickly. "Paulo, Calvin! Go to the right and swing in." He turned and signaled to Top and Blue. "You guys do the same on the left."

Krashchenko, desperate and shocked, had but one idea on his mind at that particular moment: Escape!

He cursed and kicked the three enlisted men ahead of him. At the same time he grunted orders at Deintz. "Cover the rear! Cover the rear!"

"But, *Tovarisch Podpolkovnik!*" Deintz protested. "You are going toward the rear."

"Idiot! I am moving forward," Krashchenko said. He pointed toward the Black Eagles. "That way is now the rear."

Deintz, obedient, turned around and faced the men that were now rapidly approaching him. He heard a movement to the right and swung his AK47 in that direction.

Unfortunately for him, Ray Swift Elk suddenly appeared on his left. Ray shot once, the bullet punching into the East German's neck. Deintz dropped his weapon and fell backward. He sat up, and looked up at the man who shot him.

Now Calvin Culpepper came in from the left side.

Deintz looked at him, then back at Swift Elk. He licked his lips, and spoke in accented English. "I think you fellows may have won this match."

Calvin was in no mood for bullshit. His mind dwelt on the deaths of Hank Valverde, Doc Robichaux, Dean Fotopoulus and Sparks Johnson under his command. He raised his rifle.

"Hey, you, Buffalo Soldier," Ray Swift Elk said. "Are you going to execute a helpless man?"

Calvin hesitated, then lowered the muzzle. He glared at Deintz. "I guess I wouldn't be a very good soldier in your army."

Malpractice McCorckel now appeared. He'd finished with Archie and had come forward to join his team. He quickly forgot about it as he tended to the East German. He checked the man out, then applied a field dressing. "Superficial neck wound, but the bullet busted his jaw." He stood up. "We got a prisoner, boys."

Back up at the front, the four man pincer movement pulled off their manuever and closed in with M16s blazing.

The three Red Bears went down snarling and fighting, but they died just the same. Krash-

251

chenko whirled around and ran blindly back in the opposite direction.

Falconi leaped out in front of him, his .45 pistol at the ready. *"Prival, Podpolkovnik,"* he commanded in perfect Russian.

Krashchenko stopped and looked into the American's face. "Ah! You are Falconi, of course."

"Of course," Falconi said continuing to speak the Russian language. "And you would be my opposite number."

"Lieutenant Colonel Gregori Krashchenko," the Russian said introducing himself. "I have been following your exploits for a number of years."

"So I understand," Falconi said. "But I had not heard of you until this mission."

"Would you be flattered to know that long ago I was detailed to destroy you and your men?" Krashchenko asked. Here, at last, was the individual who had brought him disgrace and nearly caused his execution. Cold rage flowed through the Russian's psyche. "We are countrymen— blood-brothers, *nyet?"*

"Nyet!" Falconi snarled. "My family in Russia were Jews. It seems that the population under both the czars and the communists hardly considered them human."

Krashchenko smiled. "That is one policy of the pre-revolutionary government that the modern Marxist system carries through, you Jewish bastard." Suddenly he lost his cool. "You stinking *Evrei!"* He swung up the muzzle of his AK47.

Falconi's pistol barked and bucked in his hand

twice.

Krashchenko was kicked into a doubled-up position by the three slugs as they slammed into his body. He went to the ground face first.

Falconi gingerly rolled the man over. "*Dosvidaniya*, asshole."

Sergeant Major Gordon had watched the encounter. Now that the formality was over, he got back to work. "Sir," he reported. "We've counted up the enemy dead. We know for sure that the Red Bear Detachment is destroyed. There's also a side development that is most interesting. It seems we have a prisoner."

Falconi was interested. "Yeah? Who is he?"

Top shook his head. "The sonofabitch is tough. He won't say nothing. Not even name, rank, serial number and date of birth."

"Piss on him," Falconi said. "Let SOG G2 sweat that shit out of him back at Peterson Field." He looked around as the surviving Black Eagles crowded in on him. "This campaign is over. Let's go home."

Epilogue

The three women stood close together for support as the C-130 approached Peterson Field from the north. It was just a speck in the sky, but they knew exactly which flight it was.

Andrea Thuy, Betty Lou Pemberton and Jean McCorkel gave each other smiles of encouragement as the aircraft flew in closer and lower for a landing.

Chuck Fagin paced restlessly nearby. "What're you crazy broads acting worried about? We already got the word that your guys are all right."

"All right?" Betty Lou exclaimed. "Archie was cut in a knife fight."

Fagin scowled. "The sonofabitch probably did it shaving. That's how goddamned dumb he is."

"Now, you listen, Chuck Fagin!" Betty Lou shouted. "I'm getting sick and tired of the way Archie is continually getting picked on!"

Andrea gently shushed her. "Shhh! You must take into consideration that he's very upset,

Betty Lou. Eight of the guys died. It was a virtual massacre out there. Each time they lose a man, it kills Chuck a little too."

Betty Lou calmed down. "I'm sorry. You're right, of course, Andrea."

"I have to admit I don't feel so good about things myself," Andrea said.

Jean patted her on the arm. "Be strong, my friend. War is a terrible thing."

"Yes," Andrea agreed. "Last night, after we received the final report, I calculated the rate of loss for the Black Eagles over the time the unit has been in existence. Forty-four men out of fifty-three are dead. That's an eighty-three percent casualties."

"It's all so dreadful that I don't want to talk about it," Betty Lou said fearfully.

"Neither do I," Andrea said. "But in my job, I can't ignore it."

The airplane landed and continued down the runway with its brakes burning rubber while the reversed props pushed against the direction of travel. Finally the pilot turned his big flying machine and rolled toward them. Five minutes later, it came to a halt and the engines were cut.

Three waiting ambulances had been parked off to one side. Now they moved off toward the rear ramp of the airplane as it was hydraulically lowered. Nine Black Eagles walked down to the concrete and formed two lines. Men from the ambulance took stretchers from their vehicles and went up into the big plane. Falconi's voice could barely be heard at that distance:

"De-tachment! Tinch-hut! Pre-sent, arms!"

With their M16s at shoulder arms, the Black Eagles rendered sharp hand salutes.

Then, one at a time, eight bodybags were solemnly removed and placed into the waiting medical trucks.

A final stretcher, bearing the wounded Red Bear, was taken and placed in a special ambulance in which a pair of MPs were riding.

The convoy's engines were started, then the group drove away.

Falconi turned the men over to Sergeant Major Gordon while he and Lieutenant Swift Elk split off from the group to join Chuck Fagin who was waiting for them under one of the C-130's large wings.

Top marched the detachment up to where the three women were. He halted them, then barked out, "Sergeant McCorckel! Private Dobbs! Fall out!"

The two men stepped out of the detachment and walked up to embrace their women. Top winked at Andrea. "Falconi shouldn't be long with Fagin."

"Thank you, Top," Andrea said. She watched the detachment march away, then turned her eyes back to her lover.

Peterson Field seemed unusually quiet for that time of day.